At God's Mercy

L. L. Fine

Edited by Julie Phelps

TO MY LATE GRANDPARENTS,
HELENA AND MENDEL FAINTUCH
AND MY OTHER 6 MILLION RELATIVES

CONTENTS

Acknowledgments vii

1 Wartime 1

2 Brothers 7

3 Meeting 19

4 Tish 31

5 Nightmares 49

6 Nabradosky 59

7 Ghosts 81

8 Lies 109

9 Revelations 131

10 Requiem 153

11 Epilogue 171

ACKNOWLEDGMENTS

First of all, I'd like to thank my editor, Julie Phelps, for her wise advice, great knowledge and skills; my wife, for without her none of this could have happened; and my kids – for giving me hope in dark times. All the events, names and places described here are completely fictitious.

<u>Wartime</u>

"Out of the mouth of babes and sucklings hast Thou founded strength: because of Thine adversaries; that Thou mightest still the enemy and the avenger..." (Psalms 8:3)

She could still make it.

Maybe.

The frozen tree branches whipped her, but did not slow her down. She could make it. She could. Right left, right left. Pam pam, pam pam.

Her feet sank deep into the snow, beating against the fallen branches. It hurt, but maybe she still had a chance. The war was over, and the area was... friendly?

Run far enough, fast enough, and maybe you can still save yourself! And the children. Most importantly.

Right left, right left. Pam pam, pam pam.

The air burned her lungs, and the small wicker basket, in which the twins lay, weighed on her hands, her shoulders, her back. She corrected her grip, held it to her body and clutched it tighter. Close to her chest, close to her soul.

Pam pam, pam pam. Right left. Pam pam.

Arms ached. Hands screamed. But she did not listen, she did not give in to the demands for relief from her hands, her legs or her lungs. No time for that. Not now. Currently there was only one goal: to get to the other end of the forest. Escape. Escape.

She deliberately chose the longer route, more entangled. She deliberately gave up the temptation of the easiest path that was more suited for her light shoes. And now she was between the dripping leaves and the frozen ground, running more and more slowly, being careful of beating branches and tricky roots. She must not fall. She must not stop. Behind her...

But she did not look back.

*

Death chased behind her, armed with a well-oiled hunter's rifle. He was heavily dressed in peasant boots, well-tailored gray wool trousers and a winter coat of a rough cowhide. Death knew his way around this forest less well than she did, but still enough to figure out where she escaped to.

The road. She was trying to reach the safety of the road.

2

He went on, cursing the past three years, in which he'd neglected his daily training and nourished a farmer's belly.

Occasionally he saw flashes of blue nightgown between the branches, and knew he was closing in on her.

How did she get away from me anyway, to begin with?

He did not want to admit the answer. He did not want to think at all. He was Death, and his goal was death, and nothing else mattered now. He knew what he needed to do.

Right left, right left, pam pam, pam pam.

The pursuit continued.

*

The echoing shots still barked in her ears, especially that splash which passed her face as she left the cabin. The same splash that ruptured a part of her left cheek. Was it still bleeding? She did not know. Right left, right left, pam pam, pam pam.

Gasping heavily, she looked down at the twins. And they, in return, looked back at her with a round and trusting gaze. Why was mother taking them out for a run in the woods? They did not know. And so they lay side by side, watching their mother panting in pain, and thinking babies' thoughts in the fragmented Polish which had begun to take shape in their minds.

Right left, right left, pam pam, pam pam.

Had she lost him?

Had Death wandered off in the other direction, in the frozen woods?

She had not heard his voice for a few minutes. In a sudden decision, welcomed by her wheezing lungs, she slowed and came to a stop. Listening.

Silence.

*

Death looked around, lacking direction, left and right. He listened as well.

Only frozen trees, silent.

3

No trace of sound, not even a hint of a blue nightgown.

Where could she be?

The forest was silent, looking at him with blaring calm. He cursed loudly, and took a few more steps. Suddenly he was in a totally unknown place. Where was the road? Where was Helena? Where were the children?

Where should he go?

Quiet.

Silence.

Not a trace of sound, nor a hint of the blue nightgown.

By impulse, Death cocked the gun in his hand.

*

The shot slapped the twin's ears violently; until now they had actually quite enjoyed this odd trip. With their mother petrified, holding the remains of her breath, they responded the only way infants respond to a slap.

Helena looked at them with growing horror. Close to exhaustion, she gathered them into her lap and tried to calm them.

Quiet!!! He will hear you!!!

To no avail. Her anguished face, pleading silently, only made them whine even more, loudly. They cried and cried, hard and sore. Suddenly they realized something was wrong. The trip was not just a trip. They cried. Because it was cold. Because it was dark under the trees. They cried because they had cried before, and they cried because Death was very near.

A wandering thought crossed her mind...

There is no chance... maybe you should save yourself? Maybe leave them behind... and run for life, for freedom, to the...

She waved the thought aside, and began to run again, the twins in her hands, howling, calling and crying.

Pam pam pam.

*

4

Death was close behind her. He saw her more and more in between the trees, her blue nightgown standing out among the gray and green. He increased the pace and closed the distance quickly.

And she heard him. Behind her, she smelled him, felt him closing in, a predator.

The road was close. But not close enough. Her fast running at the beginning had now faded to a desperate limp. Her feet inside in the torn slippers began to freeze and lose feeling. Sweat made the nightgown cling to her skin, cooling her down with paralyzing stagnation.

And his footsteps behind her. So heavy, so close.

Defeated, she stopped.

A few meters before the edge of the forest and the beginning of life, she collapsed to her knees, the basket still clutched to her body, barely breathing, blowing out in pain.

Death stopped behind her, panting slightly. Slightly smiling. Between the crosshairs of his rifle sight, he watched her get up slowly, turning around. She looked at him, and with a desperate plea raised the basket slightly.

Would he dare to do this? Could he...

He shook his head almost imperceptibly. Slowly, painfully, she turned and hobbled to the edge of the forest, to the open road.

For a few seconds she toyed with the idea of leaping out into the light - and maybe even escape - but her heart knew there was no chance. Death would come quickly, it would take all three of them, not just her.

*

The sun shimmered for a moment in the gaps between the clouds, illuminating each twin's face like a radiant halo, turning off their crying, smiling at them. And they smiled back, washing Helena with a wave of pure, childish love. A light shimmer from the chain she was wearing captured their eyes – they had not ever seen before that golden Star of David.

And Helena softly kissed each of the twins on the forehead, blessing them - for the last time – a goodbye - and laid them gently on

5

the road. One final look, her heart breaking - and she returned to the dark forest, to Death who waited for her with a cocked gun.

She approached him boldly, without worry and without fear. Decisively. Even just four meters away - a distance which was enough to deter her in the past - she pushed on, forcing him to retreat a step. Her black eyes burned holes in his face while she continued to move forward, another step and another. He backed away, almost frightened, unable to look at her face. Another step, another step…

*

A loud shot shocked the dark forest again, a flock of birds escaping the treetops.

And near the road, alone in their basket, the twins began to cry again.

Brothers

"Then the LORD said unto me: 'Out of the north the evil shall break forth upon all the inhabitants of the land." (Jeremiah 1:14)

Death.

For most people, this happens only once in their life.

But for Rabbi Jeremiah Neumann, things were a little different. And how could they not be? He was the main person responsible for the deaths in his community. He was chief rabbi for several hundred good Jews, spanning several blocks south of Brooklyn. Not really Orthodox Jews - they had their own man responsible for death. Nor were they conservative or reform, but "light orthodox". Clearly not religious - but still requiring rabbinical presence in their lives.

And in their deaths, of course.

And oh - oh, how they died. Jews, it seems, die a lot, apparently. Jeremiah used to joke about it with himself. But behind the joke was a truth not so sweet. His community was getting older, getting smaller. Every person who died took a small part of Jeremiah's soul, his memories, his life, with him to the grave.

The old neighborhood was gradually becoming abandoned; red brick buildings were slowly emptying of their Jewish inhabitants. Where did they migrate to? Manhattan, Long Island, even New Jersey drew the young and the old – oh well, old people go where old people go.

And so it happened that last winter day of the second millennium's end. For the umpteenth time Jeremiah stood in the rain, to pray-cry over someone else that died. Another piece of history disappeared, another chapter in his life came to an absolute end.

"*El malei rachamim...*" he cried that tearing funeral prayer up to the cloud-filled sky, squeezing pain and sobbing gasps from the audience who accompanied the honorable deceased on his way to the last abode of the world below.

"... *Shochen bameromim...* "

The prayer song battled fiercely against the wind, and the ancient Hebrew words filled the immediate surroundings with a sacred atmosphere of deep pain - and easy comfort, of acceptance of fate.

Jeremiah had practiced it well, but he never managed to stop the tears from bursting from his eyes. They were real, his tears, so real, so bitter, he often wondered where they came from. But where was that emptying well from which the soul draws her tears, and a man his pain?

Jeremiah did not know.

But he continued to manage the funeral service, singing aloud the last clear prayer with a clear tenor voice, and his tears mingled with the rain, running down the edge of his hat and wet his graying beard.

And the ceremony continued.

And the ceremony died.

Finally, when the last of the family stayed, weeping, facing a fresh grave Jeremiah allowed himself to wander into the main building of the funeral home, where he washed his hands and face, purified himself and went to the parking lot.

His car, a two-year-old Honda Civic, was waiting alone in the center of the lot. The rain intensified as he approached it, and Jeremiah accelerated his pace and finally slipped inside, closing the door quickly against the drops.

He glanced at the seat next to him. Yes, the tape was still waiting for him there, along with the military envelope in which it arrived a few hours ago. Jeremiah sighed softly. Really, of all days in the world... they could not break into the car today? What a world... what he would give now for this tape to disappear from his car, disappear from his life, disappear from... never mind. He started the car and began to sail slowly over the wet asphalt driveway. For a moment he considered the tape in his hand, looking at the couple of words that were written on it, again and again.

"To father."

He put the tape into the deck, and began to listen.

*

Several thousand miles away, at one of the larger training bases for the U.S. army, Eva was packing some clothes into a small suitcase. With vigorous, economical motions she folded each piece of clothing in the suitcase, very conscious of Miguel's burning gaze. Eva smiled to herself. She loved the effect that her naked body had on Miguel. It was so... visible.

9

Quickly and efficiently she placed some more clothes in the suitcase, packing shampoo, a toothbrush and an extra pair of shoes. *Enough?* Yes, she decided, and started getting dressed. Despite it being deep winter, she did not wrap herself up in warm clothes. She loved the cold, and she functioned fine in it – more so than Miguel, for example, who managed to thaw for activity only at a certain temperature. Even now, she noticed, he did not come out from under the blanket, just sent a critical gaze her way.

"Are you sure you want to fly there?"

She chose not to answer him, and continued to choose her clothes. Her panties stretched nicely over her ass, and a sports bra covered her breasts. Now there was only the question of the pants. *The brown ones?*

"He didn't answer you, did he?"

Very true. She had expected at least a phone call from him, telling her that he had listened, that he understood, or that he did not understand, that she was invited, or just that she could go to hell. But the call never came. And it bothered her. She was ready for a fight with her father, but ignoring her? That was a real dirty trick.

She recalled how difficult it was to write that letter. How stupid it was to write it. She remembered how the paper absorbed all the grief, all the emotion, till the pen simply refused to write over it. She remembered how she crumpled it into a wet ball, and decided to record herself instead. That was not easy. Though all in all, what she did she say? That she had graduated from medical school? That she was now a military medical officer, and going to specialize in emergency medicine? This was such an innocent announcement! So natural (*who am I kidding?*) for a mature American girl who wants to work in a fascinating profession and announce it to her family...

To her father.

So she added a few more things on the tape. A few little things... but so charged. *Trust your daddy, the honorable rabbi, who knows how to hear between the words. Who knows how to listen about Miguel, about Germany... you cannot hide it from him.* She did not want to hide from him.

So she went on getting dressed.

Miguel continued to assess her with his brown gaze, investigating. He raised himself, half sitting in bed, still not quite ready to get up. Anyway, she thought, he'll have to wait until the water heats in the

10

boiler. She had used every drop of hot water, every last drop. Finally, she turned to him, her shirt half unbuttoned.

"Miguel, I have to fly home. At least once. I must see him before we leave. Spend the Sabbath with him."

"I can still come with you, you know."

She could not help but blurt out a half sad giggle. Her father was not a violent person, never raised a hand to a fly... but if he saw Miguel   in   his   home?
She gave the other half of a giggle, and Miguel smiled back at her.

"Ultimately, it will happen."

"Ultimately, we will die," she gave back.

She finished buttoning the shirt and wore a light sweater over it with a heavy coat. The suitcase was organized, everything was in place... documents, certificates... she patted her watch involuntarily (there) the man's wallet that was in the coat (there) and her pendant (a golden Star of David, also there).

Everything was in place. Everything was settled. She went to the bed, leaned over it, and planted a complex explosive kiss on Miguel, a kiss that left him with damp face and smiling lips with that look foolish men have in these situations.

"I'll be back soon," she said, turned and left the room.

The hallway was significantly colder than the room and she welcomed her decision to take the heavy coat. New York in December was a very cold place. Even for her. She walked down the hall and started descending the stairs that led from her quarters and eventually off base.

In her mind, she was already in Brooklyn for dinner at home with father and mother and her sisters... she smiled as she thought of them, and a warm feeling spread through her chest. How long since she had seen them? A year? A little longer. Them, and her father.

I wonder how he reacted when he heard I'm flying to Germany with Miguel.

*

But she did not know, she could not have known, as Jeremiah never heard her tell him about it. He pulled the tape out long before the part where he was supposed to hear about Eva's expected trip to

11

Germany for her residency in emergency medicine, her successes, the college graduation ceremony at which he was not present, her military graduation at which he was also not present - and Miguel, who was at both.

He took the tape out abruptly, and although the rain was now pouring down, he opened the window and threw it the hell out. A few seconds later, a bus destroyed it forever.

*

Jeremiah came home after a few hours, welcoming the red, traditional buildings of Brooklyn. He even found a parking space close to the entrance, which certainly marked the beginning of a successful evening, more promising than the day had been.

Jeremiah hated to bury people.

He skipped up the stairs to his apartment, five stairs up to his home, not large, where he had lived in the last twenty years. He loved the feeling of returning home, the aromas of his wife's cooking, the laughter of the girls, the light, the bookshelves. He had a simple apartment with simple furniture, unpretentious - but the apartment to which he was proud to return every single day.

It was his home, which was more than enough.

He opened the front door, and the fragrance grew stronger, well-seasoned with the voices of the little female chorus he nurtured. The great dining table greeted him with a white table cloth, displaying blue pottery, and some steaming dishes on the table.

Yes, it was going to be a very successful evening.

*

After the gefilte-fish, Cholent and two glasses of wine, Jeremiah sat back and looked lovingly at his little choir. The lights were bright, the sounds were happy, and the conversation flowed and removed all traces of the beginning of his day. Hannah went to the kitchen to get the compote, leaving Jeremiah for a few seconds alone with the girls.

"So, Rachel, how was school today?"

12

Rachel, eleven years old, smiled at him with her mouth full. She quickly swallowed what was in her mouth, but not fast enough. Leah, her mirror image, replied for her.

"She doesn't want to go to the 'Daughters of Jacob' anymore!"

Rachel's eyes bulged at her sister's words. Rebecca, nineteen, and sixteen-year-old Sarah could not help but pause over their food and focus on Rachel, who suddenly became very red.

"Shut up!" Rachel screamed a whisper and glared at her sister with an expression bright with blame

But Leah only stuck a naughty tongue out at her, happy that she got Rachel in the mire. She looked at her father keen to see how he would scold Rachel, but...

"Leah! Why do you speak?"

The smile was wiped from the girl's face, and for a moment the twins looked identical in almost everything, from their expressions to the exact shade of blush.

"But she doesn't want to! She wants to study with boys..."

And Jeremiah pounded the table hard, shaking all the utensils, stopping Leah mid-sentence.

"It seems to me *you* are the one that does not want to go there, Leah! Do not embarrass your sister in public. Have you forgotten?"

Now it was Rachel's turn to smile. Mother and Father *both* angry at Leah, who had tried to get her into trouble? It was better than a dream come true.

"Okay, but Rachel says..." Leah tried to redirect their parents' attention to the real issue, which they must attend to!

But Jeremiah just got more angry. He painstakingly turned and looked grim, as if he was teaching in 'the room'. The smile disappeared from his face and his voice became flat, monochromatic, commanding.

"What Rachel says is none of your business. Tomorrow is Friday, and we'll talk about it then. Now apologize to your sister."

Leah, in a last attempt to avoid the shame of apologizing, looked into Hannah's face, pleading to her mother. But Hannah looked back at her firmly, allowing no room for compromise.

Slowly she turned her head in Rachel's direction, who sat and tried hard not to smile. Leah was completely red when she nicely asked forgiveness from her sister. From the other side of the table, Hannah caught Jeremiah's eye and thawed him with a soothing smile. He, in return, began to lightly chuckle, looking up to the heavens.

"I have raised and brought up girls... and twins no less!"

The soft giggles around the table calmed the atmosphere. Even Rachel and Leah went back to smiling as usual, but a keen eye would reveal the painful, raging kicking war that went on under the table.

*

An hour later, Jeremiah finished reading grace, and the girls were busy clearing the table and washing the dishes. The daily thoughts that had been pushed out for a few hours came back to him, and he sank into a pensive state, thinking about today's funeral. A world going, disappearing, he thought. Disappearing.

A gentle touch brought him back home.

"Hard day at work?"

Hannah always knew how to read him like an open book. He smiled at her and shrugged. Not much one could do. Work is work, especially this work of his. Strange - you can quit most jobs. *But not if you are a rabbi.*

"So, what about Eva?"

Oh, that was a subject he did *not* want to discuss. His wife had given him the tape - she always took care of everything related to the follies of this world, including mail - and he had no shadow of a doubt that she had heard it before he did. Something like that. Eva was always daddy's girl, until...

"Eva. Remind me, who is that?"

The caressing hand was gone from his shoulder, and then returned. "Jeremiah..."

For a very long moment a deep silence connected them together. Hannah gave him her warmth through her hand, but could not melt the paralysis he experienced every time they discussed the 'case' of their first born.

"She needs you."

14

"She doesn't need anyone. She has the military… she'll be a doctor! She has that Latino of hers… she'll forget everything we taught her, her family, the…"

"Jeremiah!"

The silence was now deeper, muddier. He lowered his eyes to the floor, unconscious of his drift. Hannah was right, of course. Although she said nothing.

"You've got mail." She wisely changed the subject – again - and handed him a bunch of opened envelopes, sorted in order of importance. The top envelope was actually closed, which was unusual. Hannah did not go through its contents. But she knew where it was sent from.

"I didn't know you had medical tests," she motioned toward it with her finger.

Jeremiah took the envelope and looked at it a very long time before he spoke. He had weathered many storms before, but this was something different. This envelope… there was something familiar about it. Not déjà vu… but similar. Just like a car gear that fits well, as it did hundreds of times before. Jeremiah could almost hear the 'click' of the life cycles, deep, inaudible, but clearly felt. Had he already received this envelope before? No, but he always knew it was coming.

There was something wrong with it. Something very, very bad… but not just that. His hand shook a little. Even his voice did.

"I didn't. Certainly not at Mount Sinai hospital. Never been there…"

Nevertheless, the envelope was from that prestigious hospital. It was still throbbing in his hand, keeping its secret to itself. With an uneasy heart (*why?*) he began to open it, breaking the seals with unneeded care.

Inside the envelope was a formal and dry letter, as expected from a hospital letter.

He read a few lines and stopped. He crisscrossed over the beginning of the letter and then scanned down again. And back up. His heart began to beat like a madman, hot and cold waves washed over his body. He tried to read more, but could not. Dazed and blinded, he hid his face in his hand, and thrust the letter in Hannah's general direction.

Hannah took it with a very troubled look. She did not understand her husband's response, and frankly – she had never seen him like this before. Or, not, at least, since Eva announced that she had joined the military. She took the letter, and while keeping a watchful eye over Jeremiah, began to read it aloud.

"*Dear Mr. Neumann, we hope that you will agree to cooperate with a case that we are researching about twins who were separated in childhood...*" Her voice trailed off.

Jeremiah sat on the chair, his shoulders shaking uncontrollably. He was barely breathing. Hannah put her hand on his shoulder, trying to calm him.

"What twin? You don't have a twin brother..."

Yet somehow he had.

He knew that. He had known that all his life. Jeremiah recalled all those fragments of distant dreams, the inexplicable feeling that there was someone... that he wasn't alone in this world. True, his adoption papers, which he dared to open only after he was ordained, said nothing about a brother. But he remembered him! The brother. He knew it, a brother. He was alive, this brother. And now... and now...

"This paper says that I have."

"But... this is ridiculous..."

"Please, Hannah..." and he took her warm hand in his fingers, which suddenly became very cold and numb. He looked at her, unable to say more, looked at her and the letter in her hand and then looked at the phone in the corner of the room. He looked from her to the phone again and again.

She went to make a call.

But before she got to the phone, he escaped from the living room to the study.

*

If there was a place where Jeremiah really felt at home, it was deep in his den. It was not a large room. On the contrary, it was small and cramped, cluttered with books, functional. His Noah's Ark was loaded with words and phrases, the words of God and human interpretation, amongst which Jeremiah spent his most profound moments. A

16

smoked glass door separated him from the outside world, isolated from noise, commotion and the snakes of temptation. In this suffocating study, he could finally breathe easily.

When the door opened, he was deep in the book of Psalms, reading one of the longer chapters. He read it intently, aware - unaware - of his wife waiting. Maybe she'd take the hint and leave? Or, maybe she'd take the other hint, and remain?

She waited several minutes, until King David ran out of words and a new chapter popped up in front of Jeremiah's eyes. A favorite episode would usually invite immersion in its spring - but this time it was locked shut.

Jeremiah looked up. Hannah was still there, a piece of paper in her hand.

"His name is Isaiah."

*

At the age of 27, Jeremiah had suffered from a severe case of appendicitis that attacked him unexpectedly. Was it surprising? In retrospect, after the storm and pain and surgery had died down, it turned out that this inflammation had been present in Jeremiah's appendix forever. All his life he had suffered from various abdominal pains, sometimes more and sometimes less, but never to a point when you could get a mule like him to hospital. That's how things were. *Some body parts need to hurt, no?*

It turned out to be a 'No'.

Because on that painful day, the inflammation woke up from its long hibernation and attacked him with wrath and fury. It was while reading *The Edge of the Table*, he remembered well. He was sitting, as usual, on the bed in his room, bathing in interpretations and nuances, enchanted with the web of rules woven by Judaism, when suddenly he found himself on the floor of the room, weeping large tears, crying and moaning. He clenched his fist, pounding on the cool tiled floor, deliberately injuring his fingers, just to distract him from the spinning knife-like pain in his stomach.

Post-operation something miraculous happened.

For the first time, Jeremiah felt no more abdominal pain. The wayward appendix, hidden and painful in his abdomen, had been removed, and the pain that had accompanied him all his life - the pain that had niggled so much he barely knew it existed – was gone with it.

The relief was so great. So sudden.

So painful.

*

"Isaiah O'Connor," continued Hannah, as she carefully examined Jeremiah's response to this name, that was so much like his... and so different.

Jeremiah only blinked once.

"He lives not far away. Long Island. He's also adopted. From Poland... I called him..." Her voice stretched slightly, hesitant to continue.

Jeremiah stared deeper into her eyes. And raised an eyebrow. Tilted his head to hear her words more sharply. More... reliably.

Hannah took a deep breath and continued. "He didn't answer. There was only an answering machine. I didn't leave a message."

The room was still.

After a long moment, Jeremiah asked Hannah if she also had his address.

Meeting

"Open Thou mine eyes, that I may behold wondrous things out of Thy law. I am a sojourner in the earth; hide not Thy commandments from me." (Thilim 119:18-19)

The next morning, Jeremiah did not go to the cemetery. No one, to his delight, decided to die in the previous twenty-four hours, and except for a visit to last night's deceased family to pay his respects, preparing two kids for their Bar Mitzvah and managing the routine prayers in the synagogue, he had no real obligations. So he was clear to...

Oh, yes. For that visit to his brother.

He tried to call him, himself, several times. But as Hannah had found, the answering machine answered with a familiar voice, very familiar. (*Hi, you've reached Isaiah. I'd love to hear your message.*) Jeremiah did not leave a message. Not even the fifth time.

Morning gave way to noon. Even noon did not stay long and faded into late afternoon-evening. And when it seemed that Isaiah would never answer the phone, Jeremiah decided that he could not wait anymore. Fifty years or not, sometimes the final delays of the last minutes are the longest of all.

And so it happened that at 5:30 pm, Jeremiah and Hannah arrived a block away from the address in Long Island, which was supposed to be Isaiah O'Connor's residence.

Hannah drove as she always did when they both went together. Most of the drive passed in complete silence. Jeremiah was in his own mind, moving through memories, from one imagination to the other. Despite his heavy clothes he shivered, but also sweated from stress and excitement. Another moment or two and he would meet with his twin brother. Then what? Jeremiah wondered what person he would find.

One thing was sure - he was not poor. This street stood right in the center of a neighborhood of smart villas, very prestigious. Isaiah O'Connor... such an odd name. He could understand why "Isaiah". It was probably a joke of the adoption officials, to name the twins after prophets. But why "O'Connor"? It was rare for a Jew to use such an Irish name.

"You don't think you're going too fast?" Hannah pulled him out of his mind.

"After fifty-two years? No."

"Still, you could have called first. At least leave a message on his answering machine."

"And say what? Hello, brother? Whassup?"

Hannah giggled at the exact imitation of the girls' diction. They continued to grow to be real New Yorkers, religious or not.

Jeremiah also smiled to himself, shaking his head. Hannah could sometimes be so... unsophisticated. So direct. But it was her magic, he knew. And usually - he had to admit to himself - she was right. She had the remarkable ability to read through the folds of life, directly, intuitively find the straight line between the dots. It came in complete contrast to the twisted path of the Halacha and Jeremiah's general thinking. But, again, she was usually right. Just not this time.

"Perhaps you should invite him to spend the Sabbath with us. Oh, we're nearly there," Hannah surveyed the surrounding houses. "Apparently not lacking any money, your brother."

"Money does not make you a rich man," replied Jeremiah with his favorite proverb.

Hannah looked around, and turned right.

"It's the next street."

So close? Suddenly the news washed Jeremiah with full force. It's really going to happen? I'm really here? This isn't a dream?

"The girls feel something's going on, you know," Hannah continued in an everyday tone.

"No wonder... they are *your* daughters, Hannah."

This was not the first time nor would it be the last, that the girls would read him like an open book, Jeremiah smiled to himself. They had a rare sixth sense. Almost telepathy. Sometimes one look was enough for them to know exactly what he thought, what he wanted, what he felt... especially Eva, Jeremiah thought, especially Eva...

Just not Eva.

"They're your daughters too. Here, this is the street..." Hannah's voice wandered off and then stopped.

The car slid to a halt at the side of the well-kept road. For a long moment they looked out. A white building loomed over them, frozen and powerful. Hannah glanced at the note again she carried in her pocket, just to check if the address was correct, if, for whatever reason, she had read it wrong.

21

"This is the address?" Jeremiah asked weakly.

"Yes..."

"Check again. Must be... "

"This is it, Jeremiah... "

"It can't be!" he suddenly shouted in the car.

But it was: 11th Pendleton Street, Long Island. White, big, well-kept, more than a hundred and fifty years old at least, by the style. An old colonial house, with an impressive looking large cross displayed over the roof.

*

For a long time they sat in the car and looked at the church next to them.

"11th Pendleton Street. Are you *sure* it's not a mistake?"

"I'm not sure of anything... but that's what they told me."

All the excitement, all the anticipation of this meeting, all that it meant to Jeremiah, had dissipated long ago. The shivers passed, leaving behind a feeling of heaviness, oppressive heat. Under his grey beard and black hat, Jeremiah was sweating.

And he hated to sweat

"You want to turn back?" Hannah asked.

But he did not want to go back. Not so fast. Not before he clarified some things. Maybe the letter they sent him was a bad joke, in which case, someone would pay for it dearly. They probably had the wrong address, these researchers at Mount Sinai. This, apparently, was the most reasonable option.

But it may also be the right address. Maybe they only had the address of his brother's workplace? Perhaps this was merely a mailing address? Maybe he was the janitor in this place.

Jeremiah did not know. But he intended to find out.

With a thrusting motion he opened the car door, the letter from Mount Sinai in his hand, and he got a leg out. Yes, he was going in to clarify the matter. But before that...

"Hannah... if I'm not out in two minutes, go home. Alright?"

"Alright... alright... just - take it easy, alright? Jeremiah?"

Jeremiah smiled nervously. He got out, closing the door behind him.

"How will you get back?" Hannah called after him.

But Jeremiah was not really with her anymore.

*

The church's stairs were very broad, of white marble. Along with the white walls they created a milky, clean, pure front, which highlighted Jeremiah's black clothes even more.

Indeed, he felt noticeable.

He had never been inside a church. Like many Jews, he did not feel comfortable around churches. Something of their sanctity, which is so similar - yet so different – to the sanctity of the synagogue, disturbed him. He did not really know how it looked inside a church; the descriptions he had seen were connected to the Spanish Inquisition period, a fact that did not contribute to his peace of mind.

But what it was – was big. Much bigger than the largest synagogue, which he visited often, and as he took another step he felt more dwarfed, as if he was shrinking against the white wave in front of him. Echoes of church organ music drifted through the big doors, so high were they, and the sounds of the street vanished as he walked to the (*gallows?*) temple before him.

There were a lot of stairs – hell! So many. Jeremiah climbed them with heavy slowness and increasing discomfort. Almost fear. Twice he stopped in the middle to rest. The second time he also looked back - but his getaway vehicle had gone... at his request, of course.

He was alone, and the church doors were closed.

As he stared at them, they opened, as if inviting him to enter. As if some demonic, diabolical power invited him to sink into deeper depths of the place from where real Jews never come out alive. Jeremiah froze, paralyzed, expecting a red giant at every second, full of bad intentions, with claws to rake him in...

But out of the doors came a total of three people, totally real, talking and laughing - as if they had just come out of the gates of his synagogue, friendly and warm. As Jeremiah looked at them, his heart slightly slowed its crazy rate.

They also looked at him, and with wonder in their eyes. A Jewish rabbi on the church steps? *This is something you don't see every day, even in New York.* They passed him with a skip, and behind his back he could hear them whispering.

"Did you see that...?"

"A rabbi? Here, he's probably drunk..."

"No, that's not what I meant... did you see his face?"

Jeremiah did not hear the rest of the conversation, nor did he see them exchange looks, looking at his back, and walk away. He was preoccupied with other concerns. The dozen steps leading to the church gates had ended, and heavy doors stood before him. Blocking his way.

He slowly reached out a trembling hand to push them open. The touch of his hand on the cold glass almost gave him a burn. He used more power and still more power and still could not open the doors. Was he really that weak, he could not push open a simple door?

Oh, no. He would get into this church, no matter what. Now, more angry than frightened, Jeremiah took a step backward for momentum, and intended to push the heavy doors with all his strength, when they suddenly opened again, easily. A boy of about twelve came out of them and ran happily down the stairs without noticing the rabbinic entity next to him.

Jeremiah caught the door before it closed and stepped inside.

*

The interior was very large, seeming even larger than the outer structure. The church did not have a second or third floor, as one would think looking at the structure outside. Instead, it was built as one enormous room, chandeliers dangling from expansive ceilings, illuminating the place with a soft, reddish brown lighting.

In the corner near the entrance were several hundred lit candles, and a number of people stood near them silently, some muttering, some silent, some lighting more. Soul candles? Jeremiah did not know if this Jewish custom applied here. Anyway, it was similar - and somewhat comforting. The majority of the space was occupied by long wooden benches that were quite similar to those in Jeremiah's synagogue.

But there the similarities ended. Unlike puritanical Jewish synagogues which had been cleared forever of statues and masks, this Christian temple was decorated with dozens, if not hundreds of different portraits. Along all the walls different holy Christians looked at Jeremiah, some surrounded by angels with wings, while some just looked at him with curiosity in their eyes. On the far side of the church, high above, stood a giant statue of Jesus Christ. Under it was a big pipe organ that filled the huge space with harmonious sounds, full of power and authority.

To that, angelic voices joined, thinner, belonging to the choir boys. Approaching them slowly, Jeremiah could see the devotion in their young faces. Some sang with their eyes closed, some just stared ahead. In front of them, conducting with his back to Jeremiah, stood a large person, dressed as a priest. He made wide gestures with his hands, movements blending with the great organ sounds, his movement directing the children's singing - up and down, left and right.

There was magic, great magic. Jeremiah found himself drifting, in slow and inevitable motion, to the chorus of young angels. He slowly walked up to them, drawn to the heavenly sounds. He slowly approached...

A pair of young eyes which stared out to the space behind him, now focused on his eyes. One young mouth rounded with astonishment, and stopped singing. More eyes spotted him with wide eyes, another mouth stammered his way to silence. That boy stuck his elbow in the ribs next boy, who opened his eyes - and stopped as well. Jeremiah was three feet from the conductor's back, when half of the choir stopped singing and began to whisper.

The organ stopped playing. The remaining youthful voices faded out.

The priest stopped his motions in the air. He lowered his hands and looked at them. His boys' choir, which until seconds ago flew on the wings of the chorus, was now completely focused on Jeremiah, a foot behind him.

Slowly, he turned to check the source of the interference.

25

And found himself standing nose to nose with his own mirror image.

A full moment of silence passed through the church. Two brothers, identical in every detail, except the beard and garb, looked at each other, eyes, body, legs, collar, necklace, coat, eyes again.

Then, out of the confusion and as if he remembered something, Jeremiah held out the paper that led him here.

"I got this letter..."

*

Unlike the central space of the very impressive church, Father O'Connor's - Isaiah's - study was unpretentious, clean and simple. Just like Jeremiah's, the study was very small and crammed with books, stacked on high shelves along the high walls.

Jeremiah could almost feel at home there. Small desk, cluttered, shabby comfortable chair, pleasant density - it was all very familiar. Yes, he decided, I can definitely settle here. Then he noticed a large relief figure of Jesus Christ, as if copied from the great hall.

"It bothers you?" Isaiah asked.

"No... no. It's just..." he let his voice sink in the emotional spring that flooded him, leaving him waving his hands helplessly from an island.

"Yes... it's very, very... unpredictable."

"Very."

"Even... unbelievable."

"It depends on what you believe."

And two brothers broke into laughter, a very similar one, very surprising.

"I could count on you to get smart, eh?" Isaiah said when he regained his breath.

They had not settled in. Still stood at the entrance, they could not sit down yet. But now, like an old lock released from its jamming rust, they could proceed. Isaiah gestured to the small table in the center of the room, and they sat down, sighing in the same way, in the same tone, at that point in time.

They looked at each other. With the exception of facial hair and clothes, their similarities were indisputable. The same height, the same belly. Same black eyes glistening with good faith. Same wrinkles on their forehead, the bulbous nose, and Jeremiah even noticed those three stray hairs that Isaiah grew - as he himself did – on the tip of the nose.

"Identical twins, eh?"

"It certainly seems that way," said Isaiah. "And you discovered it yesterday?"

"Yes."

Isaiah smiled, and walked over to the dresser at the side of the room. It had several unopened letters upon it. He flipped through them, found the envelope, and smiled.

"Sometimes I'm too busy to open my mail. You, probably... "

"Married an outstanding accountant," Jeremiah continued his brother's words.

"Ah... the benefits of being a Jew. You can get married."

And they both burst out laughing again, but Jeremiah was more moderate. More sad. He is Christian, I'm Jewish, thought Jeremiah. How can this be? How does such a thing happen, how can such a situation exist - the differences between them, the similarities between them.

Half a century that separated the brothers suddenly took on a real meaning. Such one can measure with clothing. Speech. Faith. They were, perhaps, identical twins. But so different, so different...

Jeremiah pointed up.

"He has a Jewish sense of humor, you know."

"Yes, a real joker up there..."

They were no longer laughing, just smiling at each other. Jeremiah felt the heat rising from his chest, golden brown and amber, liquid honey. His earlier nerves faded through his fingertips, pushed out by the same wave of happiness.

"Two brothers finding each other after... how long? Fifty-two years?" Isaiah said. "Well, better late than never."

And Jeremiah could feel the same warmth coming from his twin. It almost radiated from him. It was almost physically perceptible. Better late than never, right?

"Definitely."

"So why are we talking about it as if it was happening to two other people?"

Jeremiah thought about it long before he answered. This question has been filtering through his mind, and he was almost sure that his answer was already known to Isaiah. Still, he had to say it - if only to check it out. Or be safe with it. Yes, he knew why they were talking about themselves in almost the third person.

Isaiah beat him by a split second.

"You... you're a rabbi, right?"

Jeremiah looked at him, nodding his head slightly.

"Not only a Jew - but a real rabbi. Correct? "

"True."

But I wasn't brought up to be a rabbi, he thought. His adoptive parents – they were almost entirely secular, non-religious altogether. They did not encourage him when he chose to study Torah, did not send him to 'the room' - only after he himself chose to go there. No, he did not grow up to be a rabbi. He *chose* to be a rabbi. And Isaiah, he suspected, did not grow up in a devoted Christian family. Yes, he was sure all of a sudden. Isaiah chose to devote himself to religion, to adopt it, for his own reasons. Why?

"And I'm a priest, as you can see. I don't think it's coincidental, Jeremiah. No... it's pretty obvious. You had an absence, lack of a real family. Though your adoptive parents were there, they couldn't be a real substitute to what's in your heart. Your roots. Because of it, you searched for roots." Isaiah smiled to himself.

"Weird. Never thought about it, but I kinda knew that was exactly what motivated you. You know? You, not me. Only now I realize suddenly that..."

"... We're both far too comfortable solving other people's problems."

"Well, why not. It's much easier than just solving your own problems."

And they laughed again, sharing an intimate moment between the brothers - not blood related, but by their profession.

"So, Jeremiah, tell me - how was your childhood, what... ah... who are you, anyway?

The entire evening was before them, and the night after, and weeks and months and years. And newborn twins that fifty years ago shared the same tears in the cradle, began to share their lost years.

*

The meeting was short. Too short. Friday promised to be unique, and in the center of it was Shabbat dinner, which was going to be the strangest night ever. The rain, which had let up for a while, returned to drip over the city, and the two brothers withdrew up the wide stairs and continue to exchange experiences at the entrance to the church.

The Yellow Cab came down the street and stopped below them. Isaiah looked at it and looked at Jeremiah.

"So..."

Their hands hesitated, rounding off their first meeting. It was too little, too short. But how good – really, all so good – and not too late. Jeremiah glanced at his watch again.

"Yes... time's running on."

For a crowded moment they stood facing each other, in emotional turmoil, but motionless. They saw each other throughout their lives – growing up, maturing, happy, sad... they both closed their eyes, devoting themselves to sharing this special...

"Hey, you coming or not?"

The rude shout of the taxi driver, plump and unshaven, could not ruin the moment. After all, they would have their whole lives to come together.

They smiled at each other.

"We'll continue this in the evening. Come over, get to know your family a little bit."

Isaiah shook his head, almost embarrassed, especially in disbelief.

"This is so weird. My family..."

"In an hour. We'll be waiting for you."

They shook hands goodbye and suddenly - without warning - merged into a warm embrace, excited and desperate. With incredible intensity. From Jeremiah's eye trickled a tear.

"I'm sorry... so sorry..."

"Me too. Me too."

29

Tish

"Cursed be the day wherein I was born; the day wherein my mother bore me, let it not be blessed." (Jeremiah 20: 14)

Airports are very lonely places.

Hundreds of thousands of people pass through them every day. Hundreds of thousands of faces in a hurry, hundreds of thousands of foreigners with no time, no place. No one lives there. No one lives there or comes especially to the airport to be in it. You only come to the airport to leave again. And as fast as possible.

Airports are cold places. Strange.

Though in truth, they witness, from time to time, warm human moments. A few drops sparkling in the bustling stream, a number of candles burning in a few eyes in a sea of empty eyes. A number of separations. A pinch of consolidations. Kisses here and there, hugging. A little drama between landing and taking off, between the synthetic coffee and a professional smile.

From time to time, they do have moments of warmth.

But none of them waited for Eva Neumann that same day. On the contrary. She got off the plane into a cold New York day and an afternoon of dense winter, carried-and-dragged by a river of strangers. As if the stinging cold was not enough, her suitcase also decided not to join the rest of the world of suitcases and Eva spent thirty minutes frozen with hopeless expectation, lest her suitcase decided to finally appear on the rolling track.

It did not appear.

When it was clear that she would not meet up with her warm clothes any time soon, Eva took the long route to the TWA stand nearby. Near it a few people were having a stressful conversation with several attendants (who smiled professionally) and Eva remembered, as she rubbed her chilled arms, how much comfort the tragedy of many is worth. Finally it was her turn.

"Excuse me, my suitcase didn't arrive..."

She was cold.

*

Wearing several layers of warm clothes, a thick coat and a thick, warm aura of joy around him, Jeremiah did not feel a shred of chill as he climbed the stairs up to his home. He heard through the door, as usual, the cheerful clatter of dishes in the kitchen, the rattling interrupted abruptly when the girls heard the door close behind him.

Sounds of running, and the twins, Leah and Rachel, made a brave leap in ambush and jumped on him and shrieked, one on each hand. Jeremiah captured them in a practiced movement, and wondered to himself how long they would continue to do that.

They've gotten heavier, those two little brats.

The other women of the house were soon to follow. Rebecca and Sarah got up from their textbooks, and Hannah left the kitchen, wiping her hands with a linen napkin.

"Well...?" she asked.

Jeremiah grinned and put the twins down gently on the floor. But Rachel continued to hold his hand.

"Mom told us everything!"

"Everything?" he asked, as he walked into the living room and sat down in the middle of the couch.

"Yesssssssssssssss," said Leah. "So tell us... our uncle, does he...."

"Really work in a church?" Rachel completed her hesitant sister's sentence and both burst into an embarrassed giggle. The two girls studied their father most intently.

Jeremiah was not so pleased himself. To tell the girls so much, without asking him? Without consulting him? He turned to Hannah and gave her a scolding and questioning gaze, answered by a shrug and eyes rolled up to heaven.

Yes, of course they would know everything in the end, Hannah, but why not let me tell them in my own time?

"Church? Actually... yeah. He manages it..."

The two older girls covered their gaping mouths. But the little ones did not really understand the meaning.

"The manager?" Rachel asked.

"Yes. He is the pastor."

Her daughters' behavior did not surprise Hannah. Not really. Still, she had not expected the directness and challenge of the girls' clamor to know more. Perhaps she had hoped beyond hope that they would be a little more discreet. The suddenness of the stress made the floor under her move a little. Hannah lost her balance for a moment, turned pale and sat down on a chair nearby.

33

Rachel did not notice it at all. She was still trying to understand. "The priest?"

And Leah added, "You mean, a Christian priest?"

"Christian, Muslim, Buddhist... what does it matter, he's my twin! He's your uncle!"

The strange interlude that followed, while Jeremiah still struggled to overcome his irritation, could not break the puzzle that plagued the little girls. On the contrary. To them, it was like their father came home and told them that aliens had landed in Brooklyn. Or, more accurately, that the Lubavitcher had risen from his tomb, ridden on a white donkey and undertaken the journey of the Messiah.

"A Christian uncle?" This time it was Rebecca's turn to ask.

But it seemed to slowly permeate the girls' comprehension. Some of the color came back to Hannah's cheeks, Sarah still looked shocked but thoughtful, and Rebecca showed flashes of understanding. Rachel looked at her fingers, while Leah...

As always, Leah could not hide anything. "Ew..." She grimaced in doubt and disgust, unsatisfied no doubt.

She would generally expect a serious reproach for such a response, and indeed, even as the sound came out of her lips she realized her mistake. Fortunately, she was the only one who understood it. Jeremiah had his own words, his own thoughts.

"Well, he doesn't know he's not supposed to be a Christian. When they brought us from Poland, there was probably a mistake and he was adopted by a Christian family. That's all."

Suddenly, they caught the true meaning of things. Heard it as it should have been heard.

I actually hear myself apologizing? Do I really mean it? Is this really happening?

Jeremiah watched as his favorite faces slowly hardened, surrounding him. In other circumstances, it would be almost comical. He, the great rabbi who decides everything, in the center circle of the court, a small circle of stern and determined judges around him. A circle which usually loved him, feared him, listened to him... and now judged him harshly.

"So, yeah! He's a Christian, OK? So what? He is a family member. This is more important."

"Wow, I wonder what Eva will have to say about it..."

Now it was Rachel's turn to talk too much, and Leah hurried to cover her mouth with her hand. Rachel's eyes grew round, but she held back her instinctive reaction, not releasing her elbow into her twin's midsection. It was better, she felt, if she was not speaking at all.

But it was too late. Things had already been said, and echoed in the small living room.

*

At the airport other voices echoed, more distant, more foreign. That flight was to take off, and this flight was delayed, and a phone call was waiting for someone at Swissair booth, and the last call to...

Who cared, really? Eva pulled her knees to her chest, trying to find a position on the waiting room seat that would be comfortable and also warm, two things that were clearly impossible. Still, she tried.

Behind her the cold official clock declared she was very, very late and alongside her a large Jewish family hurried along – clearly Jewish by their clothing, with a long line of children behind, arranged by height, each child holding a child's hand behind. The father, a tall, pale creature, rushed forward, followed by the mother with the chain of children.

"Come on, come on... it's almost Sabbath... "

Yes. Soon it would be Sabbath and she needed to do something about it.

Eva forced herself out of her seat, and found that indeed it did have a certain warmth. She walked to the front TWA booth again, which she had visited several times in the past hour.

"I'm sorry, Ms. Neumann. Why don't you leave us your address and telephone number and we'll send the luggage to you when we trace it?"

Eva nodded meekly.

"Okay... thanks. Maybe I can use your phone? I don't have..."

"Of course." She put the phone closer to Eva.

Jeremiah sat in his study, trying to concentrate on the book of Psalms. But to no avail. Even King David's songs could not erase that sentence Rachel burned into his heart, that harsh truth that would not let him rest.

Eva, Eva. Why did you do this to me? Why did you make me angry with you? What made me reject you, run away from you, ignore you?

He dipped into his feelings, repeatedly considering the soft image of his eldest daughter, remembering the day she told him about her recruitment, about medical school, the head covering that she refused to wear anymore...

Her denial of what he believed in. Everything he taught, preached.

The phone ringing tickled the edge of his consciousness at first, kept ringing again and again. Jeremiah, typically, did not answer the phone. He trusted Hannah to filter conversations, and if not her, any one of his daughters.

But the phone rang again, and Jeremiah could no longer concentrate - he noted bitterly that sentence he had read five times in a row. *The girls are probably busy in the kitchen.* Jeremiah picked up the phone next to him.

"Yes?"

*

Her father's voice gave her a jolt. Suddenly she grew hot. Since when did Dad answer the phone? What for? Why now?

Eva paused. She did not know what to say. How to start. After so many months of rehearsing in front of the mirror, after so many months of rehearsing to herself what she wanted to say to the most important (yes, still the most important!) man in her life, her father's voice caught her completely by surprise. Paralyzing her.

"Yes..?" repeated her father, awakening her.

"Hello, Dad?"

Silence.

"Dad... it's me, Eva."

More silence. Then, heavy breathing, and...

"Dad? Oh, Dad, don't hang up... Dad?"

Inside the airport that was so big, so cold, stood Eva, frozen and small with a useless phone in her hand. Wrath filled her ears with ringing. She stared at the receiver in disbelief, angry, amazed. Around her, the earth swayed and the air swirled. A small hot tear was forming in the corner of her eye.

*

Another similar tear glistened in the corner of Jeremiah's eye, and he spent a frantic moment of silence in front of the silent receiver.

There was a small knock on the door and Hannah looked in, wearing an apron and wiping her hands. Behind her familiar sounds of the kitchen could be heard.

"Who was that on the phone?"

"Wrong... wrong number."

*

A few miles away, another teardrop was born in the corner of Isaiah O'Connor's eye as he knelt in front of a statue of Jesus. A flash of sorrow came over him, a sense of loneliness. For a moment he felt the cold of the airport, the discomfort in Jeremiah's throat, the burning of his own.

For the first time in his life, he was going to meet his family. Not his adoptive parents, who died several years ago. Not the extensive Irish family, not his spiritual sons, whom he saw every evening and every week. No.

He was to meet his real family. His brother. Then his nieces. (I am an uncle? Me?) All given up by him when he became a priest.

Of the three tears born at that same moment, that of Isaiah was the only one that fulfilled its mission, completed an entire lifespan and splashed to the floor.

*

Not long after, the doorbell rang at Jeremiah's home.

37

All eyes were directed at the front door. Jeremiah examined the living room of his house: clean, sleek, and shinier than ever. Not that he ever had any complaints, but... still, he was pleased to see their effort. The table was beautifully set with especially festive dishes, and the girls - all of them looked radiant and resplendent as ever, in their most beautiful Sabbath clothes.

Jeremiah felt a twinge over the desecration of the Sabbath bell ringing, but the joy of this bell, however, was actually much stronger.

He went to greet his twin brother into his home for the first time.

Indeed, behind the door was his twin brother, his mirror image. Jeremiah was amazed again by how similar they were. How the face smiling at him from over the threshold looked the same as the face he saw every day in the bathroom mirror. How their eyes laughed in the same manner. How tall their foreheads were and how equally bushy their eyebrows were (and grey). How bulbous were their noses in the exact same way, with a slight curvature to the left. Yes, a wild heat wave engulfed him, it was his brother. His lost twin brother. His brother who looked as similar to him as two drops of blood would. At least from the nose up.

From the chin down, the similarities seem hazier, hidden behind the symbols, rituals and uniforms. While Jeremiah was proud of a very thick beard, Isaiah insisted on keeping his face smooth and polished. While Jeremiah wore a black suit, distinguished, Orthodox Jewish style, Isaiah wore a white collar that stood out over his blue suit.

Yes, he was different. There was no doubt.

But he was, after and before all, his twin brother. His only remaining blood relative. And as such - he was accepted and invited to his home, in any type of clothing.

"Welcome. Welcome home."

And he held out his hand to formally shake hands, answered with the same hand and same hand press. And again, just as at the end of their first encounter, it was not enough shaking hands, and they were reunited again in a warm and sweet embrace, wrapping each other in feelings hidden for years.

"Thank you... good to be here."

The girls' eyes sparkled with excitement at the sight of their father and his twin, as they closed their eyes, hugging, as if there was nothing else around them, not the door, not the house, nothing. Finally, Isaiah opened his eyes, and saw them for the first time. He lightly tapped on Jeremiah's shoulder, and the embrace was absorbed into the moment before. The two brothers went inside, Jeremiah first, Isaiah shortly after. He walked over to the girls.

"Oh... these have to be my nieces. My new nieces."

He looked at them in wonder, their facial features so familiar, so beautiful.

"They are so similar to you..."

"And you," replied Jeremiah, fascinated.

Isaiah studied each of them carefully, and then went first to the eldest.

"You are, of course... Rebecca?"

She nodded as if she was hypnotized. The stranger in front of her, dressed in an ominous form, wearing the facial features of her father and speaking in the voice of her father... this man held his hand out.

But he is a stranger! And I'm of marriageable age...

She turned a questioning glance at her father.

"You may. It's allowed. He is your uncle."

The handshake between them was very light, ashamed. Isaiah smiled to himself. The girl was so terrified... which was understandable.

He released her two fingers, and looked over to Sarah, who stood very tense next to her older sister. She was more direct, and with a fairly businesslike tone reached forward, speaking in a voice lower and slightly older than her usual squeaky one.

"I'm Sarah. Pleased to meet you."

"Pleased to meet you, too."

And now it was the twins' turn. They clung to each other as they did often at times of great confusion, and smiled shyly.

"And you must be the twins of mischief. Who is Leah then?"

Leah raised her hand, then dropped it. Her eyes sparkled. Isaiah went down on one knee to look at both of them face to face. He took Leah's little hand in his right hand and with his left hand he took Rachel's.

"Hello, Leah. Hello, Rachel. You can call me Isaiah. Uncle Isaiah."

Their hands were warm and cute in his hand. The twins looked at him with searching eyes, as if they were trying to place their father's double somewhere familiar, in some niche in which they could easily digest his presence. And as often happens in such situations, the right thing, and in fact the only thing, was to burst out with a great laugh, the kind that solves every mystery and eliminates any embarrassment.

Isaiah looked back, not understanding, and saw the beaming Jeremiah.

"Did I say something funny?"

This question only increased the twins' giggles. Isaiah returned to look at the pair of laughing twins, and Leah caught his eye and gestured that she had an imaginary beard.

"You look just like Daddy!" Rachel explained it.

"Just a beard..."

And they continued to giggle, infecting Isaiah, who began to realize how little he understood children. Why should he understand? He had no children, and other than at church youth choir events - also had no contact with them.

Things are about to change, he thought. So many things are about to change.

"Welcome to our home, Mr. O'Connor."

Isaiah stood up, and looked at Hannah, standing at the entrance of the hallway leading to the bedrooms. Hannah was... impressive, he decided to himself. She was wearing an elegant green suit, meticulous in detail, with a designer wig (more new things to get used to) and a smiling face... but also examining him.

"Isaiah, please," he corrected the formal way Hannah talked to him. "Just Isaiah. And I am very, very happy to be here, Mrs. Neumann."

Hannah smiled a little more.

"Hannah, please. Just Hannah."

*

A dinner can be a simple thing. But it can also be an event loaded with manifest and latent meanings. Shabbat dinner was always such an event, especially when arranged and hosted at the home of a rabbi. It

40

often became a *Tish* - a real social event, with scholars who came to dine (and often sneak glances at his daughters) at the rabbi's house, with blessings before and blessings after, and a lot of unsaid words between courses.

It all starts, of course, with the Friday blessing.

"Uncle Isaiah? Aren't you going to wear a yarmulke for the blessing?"

As had often occurred in the past, Rachel's forthright manner presented a challenge for others. She was not bad - but her honesty, her directness, her delicate yet blunt way of analyzing reality around her...

Contrary to popular opinion, the devil would rather hide behind the truth. No lies.

And Isaiah, in his discomfort without a yarmulke, looked at Jeremiah, who was lost for words at that moment. He had never hosted a man who had not come equipped with a yarmulke at his home, let alone someone like... his twin brother. The Christian. And how, how did he propose to host such a strange man in his home? Suddenly the voices in the room sharpened, like a blockage in his ears was released and reality became... more realistic.

Suddenly he was embarrassed. The whole situation seemed too imaginary to be realistic, and he wondered for a moment about the veracity of these last two days. Maybe he just dreamed it? Maybe it was just an illusion, he would wake up any moment, covered in sweat, alongside Hannah?

He looked at his wife.

And she, in the most natural way, opened the drawer of the cabinet by the dining table, and without rummaging pulled out the white yarmulke, the largest one, which she deliberately concealed there before their guest's arrival. Unlike Jeremiah, she lived in a world where more than half of the people were Christians, unlikely as it may sound. And not every person had a yarmulke.

Isaiah looked at her, fascinated. He took the extended yarmulke slowly, and positioned it slowly, under the watchful eyes of the girls. It was not, of course, the first time he had put a yarmulke on his head - it occasionally happened in the church - but it certainly was the first time he had donned one before eating. Now what?

41

He sat down and was wondering what next, and about three seconds later, he noticed that he was the only person sitting at the table. Rachel looked at him with a thin smile. Yes, he decided, I'm very fond of this girl. Very much.

He got back on his feet, and whispered to her as if in secret, "What now?"

She didn't have a chance to answer him, because Jeremiah had already started to pray. Isaiah remembered some Hebrew studies and identified a number of words.

"Yom Hashishi... Veyachulu hashamaim veha'aretz mekol melachtam... "

Jeremiah blessed the wine glass, loud and clear, but Isaiah was unable to follow. Yet, when everyone said, "Amen," he hurried to join, so the ritual was respected. And as the last "Amen" was said, the festive one, Jeremiah drank from the big glass of wine and then passed it to Isaiah.

Isaiah's dilemma: to drink wine for the first time in thirty years? Or refuse a drink from his brother for the first time in fifty years? While Isaiah was struggling against the glass that was extended to him, again Hannah was the one whom elegantly solved the issue and took the glass herself.

Jeremiah looked at her, surprised, and then nodded in understanding.

Then came the blessing of the bread and Jeremiah tore large pieces from it, salted them a little and passed them to his brother, his wife and his daughters. It was time to eat, and that is always the time to be happy. But, the smiles that spread around the table came to a stop when Isaiah looked dubiously at the bread before him. *Now what?*

"I... well, I'm... I haven't blessed the food... my way..."

The family stopped eating. Naturally, all gazes turned to Jeremiah.

"Well, does your blessing contain bad words?"

Isaiah chuckled slightly. "Of course not..."

"Well... what are you waiting for? The food is getting cold... "

Isaiah folded his hands, bowed his head and closed his eyes. Soft, deep, loud and clear - just like his brother – he started to say grace.

"Thank you, Father, for the food on the table. Thank you for drinks next to it, thank you for the roof over our heads and thank you for the opportunity you gave me on this special evening, eat dinner with my family, for the first time in fifty-two years. Thank you."

Silence.

Only light breathing was heard around the table. And heartbeats. And then –

"Amen."

And it seemed like Rachel's fine voice chimed in the silence like a beaded string of light that easily joined everyone in the room together for a moment. The tension, or whatever was left of it, completely dissolved. The "Amen'" heard from everyone was great, real, and the warmest ever heard in Jeremiah Neumann's house.

"You see?" he added. "It wasn't so bad..."

And dinner, finally, began.

*

It was a fascinating meal seasoned with witty questions, sophisticated answers and sweet smiles. A meal in which every dish contained a surprise, where each bite revealed a new world of flavors, aromas, and wonder.

"So, Uncle Isaiah, why didn't you bring your kids here?" Rachel's question provoked many smiles around the table.

"I don't have any children. When I joined the church and became a priest, I gave up on the idea of marriage and children."

"But, why?"

"Well, when you're a priest, you undertake... well, you give up certain things in this world, so you can be closer to God."

Rachel raised her eyebrows in a movement filled with understanding integrated with a lot of hesitation. He was odd, this uncle. Very strange. Sarah continued Rachel's path.

"You don't regret not having a family?"

*

Looking from the cold, rain-washed street, it was not possible to hear Isaiah's answer. But you could certainly see, accompanying it, the silhouette of his broad hand gesturing with soft, circular motions. He sat just before a large window. Like the other windows in the house it was covered with a yellow curtain, through which light entered well into the cold New York night outside.

And it was so cold. Freezing. Wet. The deepest pits in Brooklyn's asphalt turned into large pools and Eva tried to stay away from them so as not to be completely drenched by a passing car. Once out of the cab that brought her there, she found a relatively safe spot, at the curb in front of her parents' house, and looked in the window. A guest was with her parents, she saw. A lone guest, but she expected to join him any minute now.

Occasionally she could see distinct shadows. There, that must be her mother, and one of the twins, and there's Sarah. The sounds of the streets had vanished, and in her mind she could hear the clattering cutlery and plates, the little jokes, the loving fights, her father's Sabbath songs. She loved them so, the same little, warm sounds.

For ten minutes she stood there, freezing in her light clothing, looking into the golden window. Finally the cold overpowered her and she crossed the road, skipping the two rivers beside the sidewalk. She climbed the stairs leading to the entrance, pushed open the doors and disappeared behind them.

*

Seconds later, she walked out and back to the street. Then stopped. Then went back in the building, took a step toward it - and stopped again. Turned. Then turned again.

And finally out into the street again, raising her hand for a passing taxi.

*

Inside the warm home, Sarah continued to badger the guest. "But still, you were alone. No brothers, sisters... "

Hannah decided that it was time to stop with the interrogations. Isaiah, however, seemed patient and smiled, but there was a limit to how much you can crucify (*and I suggested it!*) the visitor.

"Sarah, don't bother Isaiah with so many questions…"

44

"But no, no, Hannah it's okay. Ask. I'm happy to answer." Isaiah looked back at his niece.

"Yes. I was lonely. It's not easy. Though, look, I'm not lonely any more. A miracle happened to me. After fifty-two years, I have a brother, I have a sister-in-law, I have nieces... it seems like a dream."

*

Eva's ongoing nightmare was eased in the heated taxi. The driver, who glanced at this wet girl on occasion, turned the heat up in the rear seats without asking her and without speaking. If she doesn't soon get some dry clothes on, he thought, she'll get pneumonia.

But judging by the tears that washed her face, he continued to ponder, she had bigger concerns.

The taxi came to a stop at a small hotel.

*

"But, Uncle Isaiah, if you are my father's brother, how come you are Christian?" Rachel kept asking, still not understanding; she could not understand.

"Well, when they brought your father and me here after the war, he was given to a Jewish family and I was taken to a Christian family. Your father grew up as a Jew, and I - as a Christian. It's what I am."

"And now, when you know you really are a Jew, are you going to stop being a Christian?"

Jeremiah almost choked, and Isaiah paused his fork halfway to his mouth.

"Rachel!" Hannah snapped at her way-too-smart daughter.

Isaiah smiled, but this time in discomfort. These questions penetrated deeper than he expected. Too deep, too soon. There were answers, of course they were. But not one that would appeal to four religious Jewish girls. And on second thoughts, not even in the eyes of their parents.

"Ah... tell me about your school. What courses are you doing this year? "

45

And so the meal continued, more and more, one course after another, question after question. And Isaiah was lovely and forgiving, humorous, animated, articulate and patient. And after dinner they sang all songs of the Sabbath, and then ate dessert and drank hot tea, and finally - as always, it was time to go.

*

The rain returned to the wet streets again, but only as a light trickle that did not bother Jeremiah and Isaiah as they walked around the block, to where Isaiah had parked his car.

"You've a fascinating family."

"Enjoy it."

"Yes... it'll take me a while to get used to it. Smart girls. Particularly the young one."

"Rachel... yes, she does give me a lot of trouble. Asking questions she doesn't need to ask."

"From the mouths of young ones..." quoted Isaiah, and his brother could not help but smile.

Rachel's questions. Yes. She was a smart girl, maybe the smartest of his children. She had an irritating gift to see the truth without masks, to always touch on what matters. Maybe she inherited it from her mother, thought Jeremiah. From the mouths of young ones...

"Well, no one really knows what our true religion is. As brothers."

"To me it's pretty clear that you're Jewish," Jeremiah replied without thought.

"How do you make that out? They found us in Poland. A very Christian state."

"Yeah... but you're forgetting that Poland was the area most devastated by the Holocaust."

"And yet, how many Jews were there in Poland? Two hundred thousand? Three?"

Jeremiah stopped, no longer smiling. For the first time since he had met his brother, he felt something close to anger. *Three hundred thousand? How dare he say such things? After all... after all...*

"You need to learn a little more about your people," he said dryly. "In Poland no less than three million Jews were murdered."

46

And now it was Isaiah's turn to bite his lip. The numbers he had heard were lower, but now he recalled a conversation he had after seeing "Schindler's List"...

"Three million... are you sure?"

Jeremiah just looked at him, without any trace of a smile on his face. Isaiah took that in slowly, whispering in surprise. "Three million Jews. I apologize."

"Yes. Every year I light a candle in their memory. The memory of our parents."

They continued to walk.

"I never gave much thought to my parents... our parents. I always considered my adoptive parents as my real parents. They died a few years ago. I've always regretted that I didn't give them grandchildren."

"You took your path, and they respected it, I guess."

"Oh, yes. They were very proud of me."

"And yet, they were not your real parents. Three million Polish Jews were murdered, and our parents were among them."

"Do you have any proof?"

"I don't really need any."

For a moment, a silence built between them, their thoughts interrupted only by the street noises.

Jeremiah finally sighed. "Does it really matter?"

Isaiah did not answer, just smiled. He took the car keys from his coat pocket, and pressed the alarm button. One of the cars on the street answered. Jeremiah looked at it and smiled too. A two-year-old Honda Civic. *What else?*

Nightmares

"Happy is the man that hath not walked in the counsel of the wicked, nor stood in the way of sinners, nor sat in the seat of the scornful."
(Psalms 1:1)

Less than a day had passed since Jeremiah hosted his brother for the Sabbath meal. Less than twenty-four hours, but it seemed like months had passed. Life went at a different rate, and became a kind of ongoing dream. Hour dragged after hour, meals were stretched with prayers, a Bar Mitzvah followed a circumcision. Jeremiah taught, read, thought, and all he did was accompanied by a dreamy, foggy sensation. Reality took on the air of a dream. Of fabrication.

Jeremiah was aware of it, but could not find an explanation - or a cure. Even the psalms, to which he had formerly devoted every evening, began to creep in front of his eyes to turn into a jumble of unintelligible words and impressions. They played games with him, dancing in front of him, singing to him. The dream became a reality.

And his dreams wore shades of realism. Scary.

One of them, in particular, was a lively and fleshy nightmare, blood-chilling. He struggled through the darkest moments that exist just before the morning comes, accompanied by subtle sounds of a woman singing, sometimes with muddled sounds of screams and gunfire.

That woman, a huge-looking woman, was running in the woods. Running away, probably. From what? Jeremiah did not know, but he could feel the panic that emanated from her, wrapping him, paralyzing him. She ran and ran, sometimes looking back, sometimes looking at him directly, filling him with scary helplessness.

There was something behind her... something terrible, something the mind could not bear.

Under the blanket Jeremiah moved uneasily, muttering in his sleep, clenching and releasing his hands. A cold, bile sweat covered his body, and his eyeballs darting from side to side manically. While he wished he could wake up, the vision's talons were stronger than his will, and the large woman (familiar, so familiar) leaned toward him, gave him a soft kiss on the forehead, and left him. And fear blew in his ears and filled him with new strengths of loss and anxiety, culminating when the...

*

The scream was still echoing in his head, though it had not left his parched tongue yet. Isaiah, wet with bright sweat, sat up in bed, exhausted and terrified.

His breathing began to return to normal. His eyes focused, though not quickly, to the reality of his room – of what was not hiding behind his eyelids.

He looked at the clock, and as though on cue it trilled at him. Six-thirty. Time to wake up.

*

Isaiah did not sleep well that night, and it showed. He was hunched up, his eyes were bloodshot and his speech was slower than normal, somewhat muttered. The day's ecclesiastical agenda pushed through slowly, chore chasing chore, each minute running into the next.

Restless, he looked up at Jesus on the cross, watching over from above. But the expressionless marble eyes remained empty and Isaiah migrated to the largest candle table, searching for an answer within the soothing flicker of the candles.

And that is how Cardinal Ernest McKinly and his assistant, Father Mike Sortini, found him, kneeling in front of the candles, hands together, eyes closed and mouth softly uttering prayers. Sortini, in a pragmatic and brisk manner, held out his hand toward him, but the cardinal grabbed his hand midair and prevented him from disturbing Isaiah's silent prayer. Even within the church, a few things still remained sacred.

They waited patiently and after a few minutes, murmured words ended the prayer, Isaiah crossed himself, and opened his eyes. He was not surprised to see the guests.

"Father O'Connor," began McKinly, "some interesting news was brought to our attention... about, ah... hmm... your family?"

*

Jeremiah sat in his study and tried to retreat from the world, between mountains of holy books, among hundreds of thousands of important words. He held the Bible in his hands for the third time

51

that day, and tried to read a little wisdom in it. Genesis... Song of Songs... Ruth... Kings... Jeremiah...

There was a knock at the tinted glass door.

He ignored it, hoping that it would not recur.

But here it was again, a little less patient than before. His wife had something important to tell him, probably. Should he look up from the book? Maybe just one more verse, one more sente...

Vigorous knocking tore his eyes from the Torah.

"Yes?" he asked plaintively.

The sliding glass door moved quietly on its rail, and behind it waited Hannah –

And Eva.

*

"So, tell us a little about your new family."

It was not really a question, not really a command. Only a vague statement, lacking intonation, thrown out into the air in Isaiah's den by the cardinal. An innocent sentence. A light sentence. A sentence that could pass judgment on one's world.

"What would... His Holiness like to know?"

Isaiah was as cautious as McKinly was threatening, and this fact did not escape the eye of the cardinal. It was not an easy subject to broach, he knew, and the Church's position on the subject was far from clear. Although today's winds were of tolerance and love of man, who could know how they would blow tomorrow? The cardinal did not know and that did not please him.

"No need to be so formal, Isaiah. We're here on a friendly visit."

Those words flashed red before Isaiah's eyes. The last thing he needed was a 'friendship' with the cardinal. It was not good, but still - he was the cardinal. And he should be treated with proper respect.

"But of course! So, what would you like to know?"

"First of all, what are they like? Nice people?"

Isaiah hated games. Even if he, himself, was very good at them.

"They are very nice. Charming."

McKinly and Sortini waited patiently, but the answer ended, and the silence lengthened. After about half a minute of silence and two glances between McKinley and Sortini, they at last decided that a more direct approach was needed.

"What the cardinal would like to know is how they reacted to the fact that you're a priest?"

"They don't seem to have a problem with it."

"Yes, but..."

Isaiah let that sentence hover around, and then completed it.

"But you want to know if they are Jews."

Although this was really their quest, when it came out into the room so bluntly, it did not sound good. Not to Sortini's ears, and certainly not in the ears of the cardinal. They had something... unclean about them. Something too worldly.

"Well, yes," continued Isaiah, "they are Jewish. Not just Jewish, but very religious. My brother, my twin brother? He's a rabbi. But you probably know that."

The cardinal shook his head slightly. Not by much, with almost no apparent movement, but Isaiah knew the angle of his chin, and the fast blink. Too fast.

"Of course you know that. How... how long have you known?"

The cardinal did not answer. Sortini stared at the floor.

Isaiah's brain awakened for the first time since he left Jeremiah's home. *It hasn't been even one day – and already they're here. They're fast, too. Much too fast. How did they...*

"How long?"

It was not acceptable to shout at cardinals. But too many things crossed the line of the 'acceptable' in this conversation, and it seemed that McKinly understood that.

"Since you were ordained. We check such things."

Isaiah looked stunned. The cardinal's voice was soft, too smooth, ever business-like, like he was here about the distribution of funds, or other administrative trivia.

"Tell me that's not true."

But the cardinal shook his head again, this time from side to side. Tiny movements. Huge movements.

"Always... you've always known that I have a brother."

"Yes."

"Then why... why...?" his voice trailed off. And back again. "And now you're asking yourself, what about me? Did I..." And he shook his hand in the air, with a movement of instability.

"Isaiah, you shouldn't -"

"You are right!" His roar echoed through the air, and Isaiah closed his eyes and placed his hand between himself and his visitors. "You really should not."

*

Someone should have prevented this from happening. But no one stopped it, and so Jeremiah found himself buttressed on the inner side of the living room, close to the den. Eva took her position, sitting on the other side of the room, her bag next to her, and the way out to the outer door was open. The youngest girls were hiding in their rooms, and Hannah was parked between her husband and her daughter, as a mediator, reconciling, and taking fire from both sides.

Harsh exchanges. Heavy. Charged.

"I had to come here at least once before I leave."

"You left so many years ago."

"But this time it's to Germany. I'm assigned there. I even learned German especially for it."

This news took more than half a minute to be completely absorbed. Jeremiah turned to look out of the window in quiet anger. Hannah searched, unsuccessfully, for the right words.

"Germany?" she asked. And Jeremiah replied.

"And now she is going to live with the sons of the devil. What a daughter I raised..." Jeremiah's attack penetrated all of Eva's defenses, not expecting so nasty an answer. For the second time in the same conversation, she was on the verge of tears.

Hannah, it seemed, was also hurt and she responded sharply, "Jeremiah!"

But Jeremiah was completely cut off. He looked back out of the window, refusing to turn to the room, to the conversation, to the world around him. Eva and Hannah looked at him, at his bearded figure, so tormented. So hard. Jeremiah did not respond.

"I think I'd better go..." Eva finally stuttered and stood up.

Hannah went to her, took her hand.

"Eva'le, no. I haven't seen you for - how long?"

"Six years. And nothing has changed. Nothing. I thought if I came here..." She released her mother's hand gently, picked up her bag and began to walk silently towards the door. *Nothing was resolved, nothing will be resolved*, she thought to herself. Hannah stood behind her, suddenly looking her age, older, with anguished eyes, open-mouthed - but saying nothing. And Jeremiah? Jeremiah looked out of the window.

"Exactly! Go!!! Go to this goy if you must marry a non-Jew!"

Every word hit Eva's body with brute force, pushing her to the door. Hannah protected her, trying to calm it all down and stop it.

"Please, Jeremiah, don't -"

"Quiet!" he boomed, his voice thundering exactly as another voice thundered at that same moment on the other side of the city. "Go! Go away and do not come back! You're not my daughter anymore. You are dead to me. Dead!!! Here -" And with a stormy, red face, he pulled his shirt out of his trousers, ripping and tearing it apart, performing the Kri'ah – the Jewish sign of mourning for a dead relative.

It ripped right through the hearts of his wife and daughter, cutting large, bleeding wounds in them.

"No!" Hannah screamed and collapsed to the floor. She had not expected this, had not prepared for it, nor did she think such a terrible moment could ever arrive. *How could he do that, how could he do that, how could he do that...* the thought repeated itself, overriding any other emotion. *The Tearing, declaring the living as dead - were things so serious? Is...*

Eva stood for a moment at the door, amazed. Then she left the house, without closing the door behind her. Hannah burst into tears. Jeremiah opened a book and began to read Kaddish aloud.

"*God Full of Mercy...*" His cheeks were red and wet.

*

Dinner that day was silent and more suppressed than ever. Although Hannah managed to convince her husband not to fast and not to drag the whole house into mourning, it was only a small consolation. Soulful, heartfelt, normal conversations did not visit the Neumann family that evening, and during the meal there were only noises of cutlery and utensils and necessary words. Even the twins were silent, although they had, as always, many things to say.

And when the doorbell rang, all the girls volunteered to get up and open the door to whoever had come to break the mournful atmosphere. Sarah, the senior, was first to get up.

Isaiah stood at the door.

*

"They're giving me problems," he said when they both went into the den.

Jeremiah frowned.   He, like the girls (and probably Hannah as well) was relieved by the sight of his brother. Nothing like good news to ease the sting of bitter reality. Alas, it seemed that this news was not so happy after all.

"Who is 'they'?" he asked. And he answered his own question. "The...'Management'?"

"More or less."

It did not surprise Jeremiah. Rabbi and priest, members of one family, and twin brothers, it was not something that was going to be passed over silently by any religious establishment. He, on his side, expected to be summoned. He did not expect it to happen in the next week, but apparently the Catholic Church's procedures work faster.

"They don't waste time, your guys."

"On the contrary. They knew you existed. Knew for more than thirty years."

The question marks in Jeremiah's eyes were very big. Isaiah told him of the visit he had received; the exchange of words; the discovery that for decades he had been cheated and lied to; the harsh feelings that now choked his throat.

"Bottom line - all of my status in the Church, everything I've worked for over decades, is now in jeopardy."

Jeremiah nodded in understanding. Why had the Church kept this secret to itself? To avoid doubts? In order to avoid any

56

misunderstandings? So 'those' questions would not be asked? *Who knows*, he thought to himself - not for the first time, *maybe they're right.*

"You want to stop...?"

He let the question slip from his lips, just before the warning bells rang. *Stop what? Stop being brothers? Lose his family again after fifty years? But... maybe that's what Isaiah wanted.* He looked at him, and Isaiah shook his head with a sad smile.

"You're my brother. It's impossible to change that. Nor can they even if they wanted to."

"So how can I help, Isaiah?"

And the reality around them again wore an intangible hue, an unreal aroma. They both spoke again, and heard themselves as if through filters of a delusional deep sleep. Yes, Jeremiah could help. There was a way.

"I am ashamed to ask," said Isaiah.

"Speak. You are my brother."

Isaiah took a deep breath.

"Tell me... do you have your adoption papers? From fifty years ago?"

Yes. He had. And he looked involuntarily over to the bookshelf. Isaiah followed his gaze.

"They are up there... but how can they help you?"

"Our real parents. I want to know who they are."

Jeremiah smiled sadly, a complete imitation of his brother.

"They don't say anything about our parents."

"Nothing about - ?"

"No. Nothing about their religion."

Isaiah exhaled the air in his lungs with a sigh.

He had not expected that. But, on further consideration, it was clear that it could not have been so easy and simple. *What a gullible man you are,* he thought. And he was relying on these documents so much, and now, now that avenue of hope had gone, he felt an emptiness that was hard to face. Defeat, even. Did they really not have even a single piece of information? A fragment of information, any way to know where they came from?

"I'm not circumcised," he suddenly let out.

"It doesn't surprise me. They circumcised me only when I was - we were - about three or so."

"You don't think it's significant then?"

"It just means there was no one left in Poland to circumcise us. They murdered all the Jews, Isaiah. Who thinks about circumcision at all, when you live in such danger?"

Isaiah did not completely agree with Jeremiah, but he chose to remain silent. And rightly so. There was no point in philosophical debate now. He wanted - needed desperately – some real facts. Solid ones. Someone who was there, someone who heard. Someone who could prove something to the church. And perhaps even to him.

He kept looking towards Jeremiah's bookshelf where he looked at before, then looked back at the rabbi, in mute plea. Jeremiah shrugged, and went to the bookshelf. He pulled out an old folder, and opened the last document.

The first one ever filed.

Nabradosky

"How long, O LORD, wilt Thou forget me forever? How long wilt Thou hide Thy face from me?" (Psalms 13:2)

"You're lucky he's still alive."

Isaiah nodded his head, and turned right at the light. It had not been easy to find Robert White, who was listed as the soldier who brought them to America from Poland. The same White changed his address no less than a dozen times over the years, taking a number of jobs, and in more than one state. Finally, fate laughed and he was discovered right under their noses.

He had not had an easy life, according to the private investigator who located him for them. After the war, Robert White had become a construction worker, plumber, small-time electrician, and so on, engaged in temporary occupations over the years. He never married, had no children, *and when he dies*, pondered Jeremiah, *not many will come to the funeral.*

Most of those who might attend his funeral would most likely be the tenants who lived with him in the government nursing home on the outskirts of New Jersey. The same nursing home which they were traveling to at that moment.

"I just hope he'll remember something. It's a long shot," said Isaiah suddenly.

Jeremiah agreed. The chances of Robert White, now seventy-eight years old, remembering something so marginal from a war that was so far back, was slim. The very idea made him chuckle... but there was also something else even more threatening. *What if he does remember?* Something inside Jeremiah moved uneasily. He had agreed to go on this quest with his new brother, out of a sense of loyalty, but a lot of his motivation was the fact that he did not believe anything would come of it.

In moments of self-honesty, he felt it was a little like the tireless search for the Loch Ness monster. Yes: it was nice, it was even the right thing to do, and it certainly distracted him from the *real* problem he had, which was his family. With Eva. Also, how easy and pleasant it was to go hunting for monsters when you could be sure not to find any. *But what if the dragon appears suddenly, and looks at you hungrily?*

He felt uncomfortable. For a moment, he was even afraid. That feeling was a stranger to him - Jeremiah had not felt fear for years. He could not know it then, but this new feeling would accompany him to his death.

"Isaiah... maybe... maybe we should just turn around and go home? Just... forget everything?"

Isaiah was silent and kept his eyes on the road.

The old cityscape passed them and tired housing developments on both sides of the road blurred into each other. The road was rough, filled with continuous potholes, highlighting the fact that in the less affluent parts of New Jersey the winter was felt more than in other areas. Although there had been no rain for a few days, no one rushed to fix the potholes.

Jeremiah continued. "I'm serious, think about it... we can handle all these pressures. Why bother an old man with questions..." He let the sentence dissipate in the air, not believing it himself. But as he stopped the car at a red light, and Isaiah was kind enough to finally look at him, his eyes held a strange gaze.

"*Why? Do you not want to know?*"

And Jeremiah realized.

He was also afraid of it.

*

When Jeremiah was a small child, just a punk who learned at the Cheder and beat all the other kids, he would lay on his back in bed before going to sleep and watch the moths that entered the room from outside. One thing that fascinated him the most was the strange attraction, their deadly attraction, to the light that hung in his room.

It was not a special lamp, no, no! Just your average standard incandescent light bulb, yellow, drooping sadly from the ceiling on an electrical wire. But – oh, oh, how this lamp knew how to attract moths...

Jeremiah could spend hours looking at that light, watching the moths of different types and sizes. How they were drawn to this lamp, hovering around it, courting it - yes, there must be something very romantic, or so he thought at least - and finally they landed on it and burned to death.

61

And it happened time after time after time, this last moth-dance before it clipped the glass ball and cooked hotly with a sizzle. This happened time and time again, and it never ceased to amaze little Jeremiah. *What makes them fly like this to their death?* He couldn't stop turning this important question around in his mind. Could it be that they did not feel the heat of the lamp? That was ridiculous. The lamp was hot, and Jeremiah could attest to that first hand - he got a burn off it one day, when he tried to find out exactly what killed the moths.

So now he knew what killed the moths. But he did not know why they kept dying, coming to it, being tempted and getting cooked. *What, just what were they looking for in the light?*

*

"Knowing the truth. The first person used to have that choice."

Isaiah immediately agreed, because that thought had echoed in his head as well. The Bible holds so much wisdom, so much knowledge... he often felt that there was no real new, original knowledge beyond it. And not just knowledge – he wondered if there were any original "lives" since the days of the Bible. Everything humans do in life is to repeat the paths life already written, and perhaps provide nuances in its version or any other way. Like here and now.

"Tree of Knowledge or Tree of Life. Yeah," he nodded slightly. "What do you choose?"

Silence. Then, "Here, we're here."

Jeremiah was also glad to hear this evasion. There are questions that have no right answer. Or, at least, no good answer.

He saw the big government nursing home and they parked next to it. A large industrial building, which was once a hospital or school (or nursing home...) it was now used as a place where people come before death embraces them into its family. Jeremiah could smell it, the scent of decay, although the building looked pretty good, clean at least. It had the aroma that usually comes from internal departments in hospitals, and more – the smells of the geriatric ward, or oncology. Cheap detergents, medical disinfectants and the human materials that swim in them.

62

One old man, who wandered near the entrance, looked at them with dull eyes.

*

The faint scent of death intensified greatly as soon as they entered the building. The hall was the archetype of the eternal government homes lobby: too empty, too polished, too naked, too sad. A number of old sofas were scattered around the room, and a number of elderly people rested on them, reading something, playing something or doing nothing but count the minutes they had left. There was also a receptionist, and very fat clerk dressed as a nurse (Jeremiah could have sworn she was just dressed as a nurse) who was solving puzzles skillfully.

Jeremiah and Isaiah crossed the room, dragging elderly gazes behind them. It was fun. Jeremiah had not gotten used to the increased attention he received when he was with Isaiah. A rabbi? He was unimportant, but a rabbi and a priest together? That was a show!

But here, he felt the attention was of a different quality. The elderly would not ask themselves who they were. No, no, they asked themselves-

"Who did you come for, please?"

The imitation nurse looked up from her newspaper crossword puzzles, watching the two little brothers with her fat ringed, circled eyes. No one had informed her that someone had died today and certainly not two at once. For what other reason would these religious people come to this nursing home?

"We came to visit Mr. Robert White," Isaiah said.

They smiled, and the imitation nurse raised her thick eyebrows into a perfectly shaped question mark. She could have sworn she saw the old guy walking around here half an hour ago... Or was it yesterday?

"Bobby? Everything alright with him?" she asked cautiously.

"I sure hope so."

And the imitation nurse relaxed. She hated it when people died on her watch - so much mess, and she really wanted to go through her eight hours quietly. Not to mention it was going really well with the puzzles, and she did not want to stop the momentum.

63

And here he was, Bobby, in all his glory!

She spotted him coming out of the shared bathroom, pointed him out - and plunged back into her crossword world.

*

The backyard of the nursing home was, surprisingly, very large. Hiding behind the gray building was a very well-kept garden, studded with fine trees and flowering shrubs, and padded with rich green grass. If the residents still retained any desire to adhere to any quality of life, this was the place to express it.

"So - you the two little chicks I brought from Poland?" Robert White looked at them.

He was very short, maybe five feet, face wrinkled, but still upright. Armed with just a walking stick in his right hand, the old soldier led them to the far side of the garden, where the oppressive aroma of rotting old building completely disappeared. It was a place where he could breathe, so he defined it, and Jeremiah certainly understood what he meant.

Besides, during the long minutes of wandering the garden paths, he remained silent. And the brothers gave him the space for it. They told him, in more detail, who they were, what they were, why they had come to him, and how interesting it was to find him there in their own backyard, after following his trail across the entire continent. Robert just shook his head, understood with his eyes, and led them out.

To a place where you could breathe.

"You grew up," he smiled, surveying them from the feet up, and the twins smiled back. "A priest and a rabbi... many jokes begin that way."

"Yes. But this time it isn't a joke," said Isaiah.

"True. Uh... if I knew you'd become so religious, I might have left you there..." he chuckled to himself dryly.

"Why?"

Robert shrugged his old shoulders, as if the answer was obvious.

"Religion. Source of all the trouble in our world – death, hatred."

"That's not so - " Isaiah hastened to respond, but the old man silenced him with a broad, dismissive gesture.

64

"You're young, but you'll learn. Religion... it's something that leads to death. Hate. To everything I saw in the war."

They came to a bench in the yard, and Robert sat down heavily. After some thought, the brothers settled next to him, one on the right, one on the left.

"You know, when I came here, all this didn't exist?" He pointed to the garden.

"You did this?" Jeremiah asked in surprise. It was too much for one old man, no matter how talented or well-maintained he was.

"No, no..." Robert smiled. "This, the municipality did. I just enjoy it."

"Absolutely beautiful garden," Isaiah agreed, trying not to sound impatient as he was. Old people can be so... old.

"When a man reaches my age, he learns to enjoy the finer things of life."

"But... you also saw less beautiful things."

Robert looked back at Isaiah, and this time the eyes were clear, more interesting, touching reality. And despite what Isaiah wanted, somehow he did not look pleased with him.

"Mr. White..."

"Call me Bobby."

"... Bobby. We really, really want to hear what happened when you found us. And where."

Bobby sighed again. "Well, look at the two chicks... looking for roots..." Suddenly he looked up at Isaiah - and wagged his finger, threatening.

"I have news for you. You have no roots. Don't even look."

A threatening undertone chilled his words. Or maybe it was the color of Bobby's voice, which had suddenly become darker. Maybe it was the chilly wind that suddenly blew between the walls of the garden. Or maybe a combination of all three that penetrated deep into the Jeremiah's heart and filled it again with that feeling that he wanted to be far away from here, safely concealed in his safe and friendly den, with his warm books.

But Isaiah did not give up. "We would be happy if you could just tell us where exactly you found us in Poland."

Bobby moved uncomfortably on the bench. "It's been so long... what makes you think I can remember at all?"

"Don't you remember?"

And for the first time Isaiah knew, clearly, he was going to discover some of the truth hidden in this old man. *He cannot lie*, he thought. *All I need is to ask the right questions.* And he gave him a long look, quietly. Bobby eventually looked down.

"No. I won't lie to you. I remember exactly where I found you. Two small babies, crying under a tree."

Jeremiah, sitting on the other side, felt his heart leap. He felt as if he was not a part of his brother's determined pursuit of the... truth, therefore he could absorb all the layers in Bobby's voice. And he remembered. He so remembered, without knowing how it was at all possible - but he remembered that moment under the tree, the moment the friendly, young face entered his field of vision.

Suddenly he wanted his mother.

"It's important for us to know where we came from," Isaiah continued to speak for himself regarding what he wanted, things that he, Jeremiah, really did not want.

"Believe me, you really don't want to know. Forget it. You won't find anything. If anything, you'll only lose out."

"Lose? What, there?" Isaiah's voice rose to almost a cry. He was so close, almost there, and Robert White continued to play games with him! "Mr. White, this information is very important to us. We hoped to..."

"You were hoping for what?" Bobby had reached a higher pitch now, a meaty, scolding shout. Not the shout of an old man, but of a wise man. Isaiah paused, and Bobby stood up.

"What do you think is waiting for you in Poland? Only heartache, disappointment, death. You shouldn't go there. That country is cursed!" His face was red, and his hands trembled. A vein in his neck throbbed and Jeremiah feared for him, for a moment. But Isaiah continued to talk as if there was nothing wrong.

"Come on, the Pope is Polish. What could be there that's so cursed?"

Bobby slowly calmed down. Silence. A long silence.

"Do you really want to go there?"

"Yes."

Bobby turned to Jeremiah, leaning toward him, looking at him directly.

"And you – well, you really want to find out what awaits you there?"

Jeremiah hesitated for a moment, but finally blurted out, "We are together."

"Then I will tell you. I'll tell you how to get to the place you ask. I will tell you. Well. First of all," he took a deep breath, "you have to get to Warsaw..."

*

For more than two hours the old man described the way. Two hours of speaking clearly, two hours of words, burning onto Jeremiah's heart, that would accompany him for his whole lifetime. The description was accurate, like paintings, to the point. Not a curve in the road missed, no sign nor town. Like a prayer. Like-

And the old man had remembered everything, as if it was his daily walk in the garden, not a one-time campaign conducted fifty years ago. It seemed strange to them, but a week later, when they both landed in Warsaw, they relied on this description more than the trusted the words of Nicolas, the young guide they hired there – as recommended by White, of course.

"In Warsaw organize yourself a guide. An interpreter. Doesn't matter if he's young, from the new generation. Poland is an evil land to foreigners, more sinister than Russia, more sinister than hell. Especially to Jews. Poles were worse than the Nazis. I'm sure most of them still are. Anyway, you take the train to a place you know by the name of Auschwitz. Recognize the name? It's just the beginning for you. It's only the beginning.

"Rent a car there. Don't rent an expensive Western car. In Poland act as a Pole. Hire a Lada jeep – it's the only vehicle that will drink the fuel they sell there, and drives through the places you need to get to."

*

67

Boldistooik was no longer such a small town, but one look at the old-fashioned gas station and the local cars made Jeremiah love the Soviet-looking Lada. Other vehicles just seemed too delicate to drink that impure liquid sold there as gasoline.

On the way, he never took his eyes off his brother, who looked very upset after visiting Auschwitz. It was the first time for both, but Jeremiah knew the place existed, had seen photos, watched a movie or two on it. But Isaiah - Isaiah took a total blow to the head. The display cases of shoes and hair, the way in which their accusers tried to erase the world in which they lived... it was a blow that Isaiah suffered in a personal and deep manner. *Yes, yes... he is completely Jewish*, Jeremiah nodded to himself. *And so am I.*

He was particularly impressed by a lively youth group who were visiting the site. He'd never seen anything like them. Tanned children, well-built, with faces intended for smiling - but that day, in that place, they were quite serious. *These are not Polish children*, it was clear at first sight. But after they started talking, he realized who they really were.

His eyes were bright, and surprisingly a smile spread across his face. *Israelis! How wonderful...* they had not abandoned the past... not betrayed the legacy. For a moment he wanted to keep the news secret for himself, but he immediately nudged his brother's plump waist (a movement so natural, yet so strange) and whispered a few words in his ear.

They spent half a day among the buildings of this compound of death, following the Israeli group, and found themselves an object for the curious stares of the boys. One of them, a tall redheaded boy, struck up a conversation with him in poor English.

"Are you brothers?" he asked directly, and when he was given the true answer, he gave an affirmative mere nod in understanding, without asking further questions.

"From Boldistooik you travel towards Birkenau. Another famous name. Not far from Auschwitz you can stop. In Birkenau – don't. There's no point. Instead, you cut to the right road when you see a wooden sign that reads Docniah.

"It should be a country road, sometimes covered with mud. After exactly thirty-seven kilometers - not miles, kilometers! - break to the left with your jeep to the small path fit only for sheep."

Only here White's description began to break down. The little sheep trail was revealed to now be a well-paved asphalt road and the wooden sign was now well-printed on an aluminum rectangle, where it was written in red: "Nabradosky 40 miles."

The road twisted between two mountains, up and down and disappeared behind them. An occasional large truck passed them, flashing its headlights at them so they would stick to the correct side of the road. The trucks never slowed down to check if the Lada clung to the right indeed.

"Right, now you got from the map everything you know in the world, and you start to get closer to what awaits you in Poland. I know it. I went through that way in the war.

"You'll come to a rural area, a remote region. No phone. No electricity. Carry a cell phone, but it's not certain you'll be able to receive anything. Try... "

They certainly tried, and the reception there was excellent. Not to mention the line of electricity poles and telephone lines that accompanied them for hours on the long journey, and continued far ahead. No doubt Nabradosky had developed a little in the last fifty years.

"At some point the trail begins to expand. After two hours of driving you'll reach a small hill overlooking the village. No more than twenty small houses, old, built of stone. You'll recognize the place by the three huge pine trees, if they're still there."

*

They were there.

Three large trees, more specifically two living trees and beside them a wide and tall tree stump, that the years had eroded like a gray tombstone. Next to them a few small huts were scattered, ancient-looking, crudely built of stones without mortar. Some were derelict, but others still showed signs of life: laundry fluttering in the remains of the disappearing sun, a few chickens pecking the snowy mud and a pile of firewood here and there.

Jeremiah looked at it doubtfully. It was a rural environment, lagging behind the world. It was in stark contrast to the modern road which bypassed it and entered into the concrete town ahead. Nicolas - the same young guide, whom they hired several hundred miles to the west - slowed down near the old village, and felt the brothers' quiet stare. It was silent inside the vehicle, but the rabbi's and the priest's ears still echoed with Robert's last words, just before they left him. Warning words.

A clear and bland sign welcomed them on their arrival to Nabradosky. Nicolas started to say something, then saw the look in the brothers' eyes. They did not need to know more. He pressed the accelerator, and the grey town closed in on them from all sides.

"So this is Nabradosky," said Jeremiah himself.

"Yes. A new road," Nicolas blurted out in a heavy Polish accent.

"Excuse me?"

"A new road. This name's meaning."

"Oh."

Night fell quickly, and the streetlights came on. The Lada wandered the empty industrial deserted streets, which began to be washed in the rain. For more than twenty minutes they wandered the blackened roads. Except for a bunch of drunken young people, they did not encounter anything meaningful.

"Where is the hotel you were talking about?" Jeremiah asked. His voice was a little strained.

"We'll be there in a minute."

In three minutes, they were parked. Above them was a two-story building, well lit. On the ground floor was a noisy bar lit up very bright yellow. Despite the heavy rain, which grew heavier by the minute, people continued to enter the pub, swallowed up by the illuminated yellow door.

"Shall we go in?"

"We don't have a lot of choice, do we?" muttered Isaiah, and the three began to pull the suitcases out of the car.

*

The sounds emanating from the pub increased dramatically once they went inside. Hoarse speakers emitted a loud rock song in throaty Polish, forcing the patrons to shout in order to talk. Yellow light from

70

several bare bulbs illuminated the rough wooden tables that were bare
– except for a thick, viscous layer of food remains stuck to them. It
seemed to be a cross between a workers' canteen and a medieval
tavern. Crammed into the crowded room were more than a hundred
faces with long bristles and thick mustaches, simple people with dirty
hands and faces, reeking of onions and alcohol. Many of them played,
between one drink and the other, different games - backgammon,
cards, and chess.

Jeremiah and Isaiah, a little dazed by the noise and smells,
remained standing in the entrance, unnoticed. Nicolas, however, went
in, and began to speak with broad gestures to an exceptionally large
man, dressed in a dirty white apron. Following a short discussion the
man nodded his head, and pointed to the spiral staircase at the back of
the pub. Nicolas worked his way back through the crowded tables.

"Come, we have rooms," he shouted loudly enough to be heard.

They picked up their bags and began to trudge toward the stairs.
Jeremiah was not sure, but it seemed like the noise level began to die
down. The shouting subsided. Only the speakers continued to make
noise. He glanced around.

Everyone in the pub stopped what they were doing and looked at
him coldly. Cards were thrown down on the tables. Chess games were
paused. Vodka glasses froze in the air. All eyes were on Jeremiah, and
those eyes were not friendly.

"Zyd," a gruff voice came from the back of the pub. *Jew.*

Some eyes turned towards the table at the back. It was a large table,
cleaner than the rest, populated by some very elderly people, aged
seventy or eighty, Jeremiah estimated. The eight seniors sat there
silently looking at him, shaking their heads slightly.

"Zyd."

The call was repeated from another corner of the pub, and
whispers of approval answered him. The man who had entered the
pub was a Jew without any shadow of a doubt, and even those who
had never seen a Jew could identify him. What was a Jew doing here?
You never know. Was it a good thing? Of course not.

Then one of the elders took his wooden cup in his hand, took a
deep gulp and slammed it down on the table. At once the ambient
noise level returned to normal. Cards were lifted from the table,

71

soldiers continued their play, and gallons of booze poured down thirsty throats.

The pub returned to normal and the three continued on their way to the stairs. But only after the noise was muffled by the floorboards beneath his feet did Jeremiah remember to breathe again.

*

Three flights of stairs and a long walk down the hall brought Eva and Miguel to the apartment that would accommodate them in the upcoming years. The door, like every other in the residence, was simple and wooden, but theirs bore a small sign saying 307.

Eva threw their bags on the floor and unzipped her jacket. Hamburg weather was very cold and she and Miguel had to wrap themselves up in the heaviest clothes they could find. Despite the freezing temperature outside, inside the building it was relatively warm and it had been a strenuous three-story ascent up the stairs, with heavy suitcases, that made them both sweat.

"We're here," Miguel said quietly.

Eva was not happy. She fought so hard to get this job, this place, this apartment with the man standing beside her. Worked so much, gritted her teeth and fought for their right to be here - and suddenly, the wooden door seemed meaningless. Was it really worth all that effort?

Miguel opened the door with the key he received from superintendent; they entered the ordinary-looking studio apartment that almost matched the previous houses that each of them lived in, in the past. It was a room, not large, militarily furnished, with two beds joined together, a dresser, a desk and a small dining table. A small kitchenette populated the far corner of the room, and a small door next to it suggested the toilet and bath.

While Eva was surveying the apartment, Miguel had time to relieve himself of his coat and test the quality of the springs in the bed. They were not too good, but it did not bother him. He closed his eyes and smiled. *It was a very long flight, damn.*

Eva sat down beside him, pensive. She stared into space, trying to organize her thoughts. Images flashed before her eyes, distant voices whispered to her. There was something she had to remember... but what was it?

"Okay. Start talking." Miguel's soft voice whispered so close to her ear, it made her smile awkwardly. "Oh, come on. You were quiet the whole flight here. From the moment you came back from your parents' place, pretty much. What happened there? He's still not talking to you?"

That's not what happened exactly, she thought to herself. She had so much to tell, and so few people to tell to. Suddenly she realized that although it seemed that way, Miguel was not a real part of her life. Not yet.

"I have a new uncle." She said it so quietly, Miguel was not sure he heard right. "My father, it seems, has a twin brother. We didn't know about it until now. I didn't see him... my mother told me."

He was still not sure she was serious. She had a weird sense of humor sometimes. No, not the classic Jewish humor – not like Woody Allen, or Seinfeld. No, it was something else. Borderline creepy. Eva played a lot of characters for him. Sometimes it felt like there was more than one Eva, as though from those beautiful eyes, there was sometimes another person looking at him. Playing with him.

"That's... good, isn't it?"

"I think so, but it's weird. He's... Christian. A priest."

"Jesus Christ! Though... so am I…"

"Yes. But you think it helps him understand? Forget it."

*

On the second floor of the inn there were four rooms arranged along a corridor. In the first one lived Shuga, the innkeeper, who accompanied them on their way up. On his way he knocked roughly on the second door. Out stepped a woman, old and toothless, who nodded tiredly, looking fuzzy and returned to her room.

Another room, the smaller of the two remaining was allocated to Nicolas. He entered it with two suitcases, and Kristzha (Jeremiah heard Shuga address the old lady as that) after seeing Nicolas fit in the tiny room, pulled out another key and opened the room across from it.

73

It was a bigger room which had obviously been cherished some years ago. The walls were covered with old, satin fabric wallpaper, adorned by embroidered forested landscapes. Against the wall stood a carved wooden chest. The dresser was covered with white lace, and on it were scattered native porcelain dolls of peasants at work, of cows and chickens. Each side of the dresser - and in sharp contrast to it – was a simple iron bed with a thin foam mattress, bare of sheets.

Kristzha let out a few incomprehensible words, smiled a toothless smile, and left the brothers alone in their room.

Isaiah spoke first, pointing to the floor below. "They don't like you here."

"I noticed."

They began unpacking their suitcases in silence, each man for himself. Jeremiah peripherally noticed something Isaiah took out his trunk: a Torah. *We could have saved some weight*, he thought as he put his personal copy at the top of the bed, and went on to unpack his pajamas.

A polite knock on the door stopped him. Isaiah, who was closer to it, approached and opened it. And when Jeremiah identified the man in the doorway, his heart leaped in his chest again.

It was the old man from downstairs. The "Zyd" father.

Up close, he looked more impressive. Six feet tall, gaunt, high forehead, bright blue eyes, hooked nose. He was wearing slightly more respectable attire than the general drunks downstairs. Seventy years old, Jeremiah guessed. And well preserved.

He just stood there and smiled.

"Sorry, I do not speak Polish..." Jeremiah stammered the only words he knew in the local language.

"So, maybe we can talk English," the answer shot back in clear English, with almost no accent.

Jeremiah smiled, almost embarrassed. He had not expected this, and suddenly felt uneasy. The old man stood at the entrance for almost thirty seconds, still wearing the same friendly smile, waiting to be invited in. *Where are my manners, really?*

"Of course! Come inside," he gestured.

The old man hobbled in, helped by a long cane.

"Thank you, thank you," he said. "...and welcome to Nabradosky. My name is Jerric, and... nice to meet you."

He was still full of smiles, but Jeremiah could not ignore his eyes. They were cold and roamed the room as if trying to find something hidden. Then they rested on Isaiah.

"Welcome to Nabradosky," he repeated.

"Our pleasure," replied Isaiah, and held out his hand for a handshake.

"Isaiah O'Connor."

"Jeremiah Neumann."

Jerric shook hands with them both. His hand was warm, dry and very stable. A hand that used to be very Strong.

"I'm sorry that I showed such rudeness before. It's just, we are not used to... tourists here. You intend to stay here long?"

"Uh... we don't know. It depends."

"Depends on what, if I may ask?"

Jeremiah and Isaiah exchanged glances. Both had the same thought in mind, and both could read it in each other.

Jerric also sensed that, apparently, and his smile broadened. "Maybe... maybe I can help you. I'm pretty well-connected here."

Of that I'm sure, an inner voice rang within Jeremiah. Without even knowing him, he knew he did not trust him. The man gave him chills - from that first encounter in the bar below, from the first look at the door. He did not like the way he smiled. He did not like his handshake either. But, as the man said, he was connected here. That was a start.

"Maybe you can. Have you lived here long? "

"Since I was born."

There was a soft knock at the door and Kristzah came through it, hands stacked with folded white sheets, some towels, and two thick blankets. This pile of textiles concealed most of her field of vision, so she could not see Jerric, bumped into him and nearly knocked him to the floor. Jeremiah caught Jerric to prevent him falling, but the blankets scattered onto the wooden floor and one of the beds.

Jerric flushed with anger and released number of phrases into the air that sounded like a cross between commands and curses. Kristzah accepted this like an almost physical beating, her head lowering every time Jerric raised his voice. She cowered like a beaten dog, and as such, she finally raised her cowed eyes.

Then, for the first time, she noticed Jeremiah.

Her eyes widened in disbelief, and then what looked like fear... or something like it. She crossed herself suddenly, fervently, in a state of great excitement, and began to murmur in Polish, with the words *Santa Theresa* repeatedly woven into her words.

Jerric was furious. He breathed deeply and powerfully barked more commands in Polish at Kristzah.

This had an immediate effect. Kristzah stopped short. She quickly gathered up the scattered sheets in the room, and laid them on the bed. All the while Jerric stood over her, monitoring her movements, and the two brothers just stood there, too confused to speak. Still, they noticed how Jerric's face hardened and froze.

Kristzah finished placing the sheets and fled from the room. Like the wave of a magic wand, the smile was back on Jerric's face, and he turned back to the brothers, apologetically.

"Forgive Kristzah... villagers here still need to learn some culture."

"I thought you said that you're from here too?" Isaiah said dryly.

"Definitely. But I also went to university, I studied languages... I know something of the world."

"Then you'll certainly be able to help us. We're interested in the history of the town. Especially during World War II."

The smile on Jerric's lips froze - very slightly - but it was noticeable.

"World War II. Why?"

Jeremiah took a deep breath. *Should I tell him? Should I risk telling him? On the one hand... we came here to search for information... it shouldn't be such a big deal... just a search for simple information... on the other hand... there's something about this Jerric, something unclean. Should I reveal it to him? Is the question even relevant?*

The look that passed between him and Isaiah confirmed that the question was relevant. And the decision was his.

"Why, because... apparently we were born here, like you. During the war."

The words floated in the air for some long seconds. The sentence, stated this way, was given new dimensions. Its hidden meanings,

76

which the brothers had not yet realized, were given shape in the room. Not yet a precise form, still no color or outline, but it was, indeed, now formed. And it was not pleasant.

Jerric's nostrils flared. He took a deep breath and stared at Jeremiah. Then Isaiah, then Jeremiah again. He exhaled slowly, breathing the words out slowly. "You were born here... amazing. You two are brothers?"

"Twins."

"Yes... you look alike. A lot." Jerric looked at Isaiah. Surprised tones permeated his voice. "But... are you... you are a priest?"

"True. U.S. soldiers found us as babies, not far from this village. We grew up in two separate families. My family was Christian.... my brother's family..." He shrugged, passing on the obvious. Jerric kept investigating.

"In America?"

"Yes."

Jerric digested the facts in his mind, turned them over several times, and then returned to his smug manner, shook out his wrinkles to regain his magic smile, and clapped both hands together.

"Listen - this is truly amazing. So, how can I help you?" Jerric's businesslike tone swept Jeremiah along too, for the first time. His concerns, if any, had apparently been forgotten.

"Well, we're looking for our real parents. They were supposed to have lived here during the war."

Jerric thought for a moment, frowned, looked like he remembered something - and then canceled with an apologetic nod.

"Sorry. I don't remember such a case."

Isaiah, who had been very quiet until now, stepped forward.

"Are you sure?" he asked eagerly. "Maybe twins that were left alone in the woods? Perhaps an unwanted pregnancy? Abandoned?"

But Jerric shook his head.

"It was a small village. I'm sure I would remember something like that. There were no twins. Not here." He thought for a split second, and then added, "Are you sure you came to the right village?"

Jeremiah suddenly realized that they were not sure of anything. *We traveled half a world to get here, and here — it takes only a few words of some old guy to send us half a world back.*

77

"Yes. We think so."

Jerric looked at them quizzically again, further undermining Jeremiah's peace of mind. Even Isaiah, who was very animated a few moments ago, had gone flat again. Jerric saw it all. Saw and noted.

"If so, you must have been misled. Shame you went to so much trouble..." He turned toward the door, turned to leave, then turned back to the brothers.

"Anyway, if you need anything, just ask me." He breathed deeply, sighed, and went on, "A piece of advice from a friend - it's not so... advisable for Jews to be here alone, you see. Some people have some bad memories here."

*

Only after the sounds of Jerric's boots on the wooden stairs had turned into distant taps, did Jeremiah and Isaiah allow themselves to speak again.

"What memories is he speaking of, if no Jews lived here?"

"I don't know," said Isaiah. "Robert's instructions were very accurate."

"Yes, but he said there were no Jews here. That this isn't the right place."

Jeremiah was silent. The recent days had been full of revelations for him and with a wry smile he accepted the realization: *It's just me here, looking for Jews.* Isaiah, he understood, would be happy not to find any tefillin readers here. No trace of Jews would be perfectly fine with him. *And what would Jerric prefer?* It was still a mystery.

"Yes. Precisely because of this," Isaiah replied, "I think we're in the right place. Seems very logical to me that there are no Jews here, and never were."

He glanced at his brother, waiting for a response that did not come. The differences in attitude between them were clear and known under the surface, and Isaiah feared the moment they would look at them in the face. Either way, Jeremiah kept a straight face.

"Besides," he continued, "I don't trust this old man's memory. Tomorrow morning we'll go to the town records office, see what they have."

78

With that, Jeremiah could agree wholeheartedly. Tomorrow they would look into it. Tomorrow the real work will begin. And tomorrow, according to a particle of fear in his mind, would change many things in the world.

From the closed window arguing voices were heard. They were, obviously, very loud because the glass of the second floor windows had silenced most of the street sounds so far, except for the occasional drunken laugh. Jeremiah glanced through the window - and froze. He summoned Isaiah closer... carefully.

Two floors below them, in the yellow light of a solitary streetlamp, Jerric was at the center of the group of elders from his table, arguing with conclusive gestures. Although the twins did not understand a single word of the few sounds that penetrated the window, it was clear that this was not an easy debate.

And suddenly, without warning, one of the elders pointed up toward the window which Jeremiah and Isaiah looked out from. And although he did not even look in their direction, the two brothers moved away from the window quickly, hiding from view.

They returned to look after a few seconds, just in time to see the group disperse. Jerric got into an old, green pickup truck and drove away.

Ghosts

"The cords of Sheol surrounded me; the snares of Death confronted me." (Psalms 18:6)

That night, his first in Nabradosky, Jeremiah could not sleep. He turned from side to side, scrambled between shattered dreams and reality, wandering between visions and nightmares. Only towards morning did fatigue overwhelm him and he plunged into an old dream, this time more powerful than ever. Clearer. Sharper. Continuous flashes of vivid color and prickling sounds.

The dream was familiar. He had dipped into it several times before, but this time it was all a bit different - fuller, deeper, just as a knock on a hollow wall is different from a knock on a solid wall. More real. Closer. Important.

Jeremiah was once again in a big basket in the small cottage, lying with his brother under a huge wall, roughly plastered. The thick wooden door let in a light mist as it closed behind his mother. Yes, the woman with the sad face, familiar, which he knew so well – and did not know at all.

She looked at them, sad as always. Then there was a loud sound - thunder, no - lightning. And another followed, and another. The sad look turned to a frightened glance out, and when his mother's eyes returned to him, they were different - wider, more alert. Frightened.

She tried to tell him something, but the sounds were too loud, and she could not be clearer. He willed her to raise her voice and she, from afar, tried to overcome the cries and thunders, trying harder and harder to reach him. He stared into her eyes, trying so hard to hear her words.

Tears came to her eyes, and she came over and hugged him. The noise was too loud for him to hear her, but the pounding of her heart had become his throbbing heart and suddenly it was he who held her, or vice versa, and the thunder grew louder, and the door opened, and they ran out.

Only when they were out, running fast from the sounds behind them, he felt that something was missing. Something important. Then he was in his mother's arms again, although he remembered he was supposed to be in a basket. Behind them. Behind them. What was behind them? What had he forgotten?

Suddenly he recalled. With a strong and long heartbeat, he looked back over his mother's shoulder, far into the abandoned cabin.

A basket was still there. A small baby, identical to him, was waiting in it.

*

Isaiah emerged from his sleep early. Something bothered him, troubled him. When his ears began to hear the sounds of the real world, he heard Jeremiah muttering to himself quietly.

He got up on his elbows, still fuzzy.

Jeremiah was at the window, tefillin in his hand and his head bowed, praying. For Isaiah, who until now had only vaguely known the customs of Jewish prayer, this sight seems very strange. A long, thin leather strap was wrapped round Jeremiah's bare hand and a large black box was attached to it. A similar box was attached to his forehead, by a similar strap. He mumbled half-speed verses in Hebrew from a prayer book.

Out of the corner of his eye, Jeremiah noticed a movement and noticed him. He smiled at his brother and continued to pray, his eyes shining.

"What...?"

But Jeremiah did not answer. Instead, he hushed him with a finger movement, and continued to pray.

Isaiah nodded in understanding. Silently, he took his prayer book from his bag and also began to pray. In Latin.

The murmurs infused into each other, with identical voices whispering different words in ancient languages, one which was considered completely dead rose and the other, more common, did not. Jeremiah and Isaiah both felt the strange harmony, the supernatural aura that flowed between the languages, between the worlds. It was, he felt, a hint of the way it meant to someone who practiced two ways of praying. Like a gear that integrates naturally into place, it felt right.

So the two brothers greeted the day, each in his own way.

*

The prayer ended and vanished, leaving behind a muddy and grey morning. The view from the window revealed a smoky, industrial, town and morning mist which filtered through and into the daily routine. Very few cars were on the street, and by daylight you could see the makeshift materials that made up some of the houses - tin shacks, bits of tree, crumbling concrete blocks.

The road, which at night looked paved, was revealed by the morning light to be a combination of tamped earth and concrete blocks. The sidewalk was well broken up and the heavy trucks passing in the street explained why - it just was wider than the road, so it drove with two wheels on the pavement. Pedestrians, mostly men even greyer than the drab fog, skillfully skipped aside to avoid the noisy monster.

Today the search will commence. But really, today... today walls would begin to crash down. *Where would they fall, what else would crumble with them?* Jeremiah did not know.

And along with Isaiah, he met Nicolas outside their room, and they left.

Outside the warm wooden walls it was cold - very cold - cold enough for snow. A cold that gets into your nostrils and freezes them from the inside. Nicolas rubbed his hands together and looked at the horizon.

"There will be a serious storm soon."

"So let's hurry," said Isaiah. "And hope that they have some useful archives at city hall."

They got into the vehicle and Nicolas started the engine.

*

The city hall was not far, and their Lada jeep was perfectly suited for the Eastern European road conditions. Jeremiah noted the attention their miserable vehicle drew. To most people in Nabradosky, the "Nivah" was a luxury vehicle, almost ostentatious.

After a few short minutes the Lada pulled up next to a square, gloomy concrete structure, two stories high. A small metal sign declared it was Nabradosky City Hall, and a smaller sign warned against destroying the flowers, or so they were told by a smiling

84

Nicolas. Jeremiah looked at the cultivated beds along the wall, where there was no sign of any flower or shrub.

They entered.

The stark Soviet architectural style naturally continued inside the building. It seemed everything was made of concrete there: floor, walls, shelves that emerged from the wall, reception desk, even waiting benches. It was as if the whole building was cast in a grey remote concrete factory, and came here fully prepared.

And the rigidity of its concrete, it turned out, seemed to extend to the rules, as Jeremiah and Isaiah discovered after forty minutes watching Nicolas fighting to gain access to documents. He was not enjoying much success, engaged in a monotone, Polish argument with a furious, fat clerk named Hans, emboldened by his thick mustache.

After the exchange of words was repeated for the tenth time, Jeremiah decided he had had enough.

"Come on, I'll show you some magic." And he stood up, took his wallet from his jacket pocket and pulled out a ten dollar bill. He stepped forward - but Isaiah stopped him with his hand.

"It's better... I think it's better if I do it."

Jeremiah nodded in understanding, and handed the money to Isaiah.

Dollars, it turned out, seemed to grow in value when they leave the United States. In Nabradosky, apparently, they had a crippling power. Nicolas and the mustachioed clerk looked at them as if the bill was taken from holy tablets. Hans chuckled excitedly and grabbed the bill, while Nicolas exhaled in amused frustration and leaned back in his chair.

"Good. You gave him about fifty times beyond his wildest dreams."

The official evaporated from the reception window, and Isaiah smiled. Fifty or five hundred times, ten dollars were still only ten dollars. And that was worth far more than an hour of waiting in this Polish dump was worth.

"Real magic..." he winked as Jeremiah came up behind him.

*

Hans arrived in the old archives humming a happy song. This morning was a refreshing change from his recent woes - the separation from his wife, the trouble with his child, the new demanding mayor - all gone with the rustle of this little treasure in his pocket. He could already taste the vodka, coolly burning down his throat. He could buy so many bottles now! So much drink-induced amnesia was at his disposal... but on the other hand, why not take the money and spend it on that same young lady, the one who was the reason his wife decided to leave? There was an interesting thought... he turned to the dusty shelves.

*

After about ten expectant minutes, Hans returned to the waiting room dragging a cart behind him, laden with five heavy cardboard boxes filled with old documents. He presented them with a smile to Nicolas, and they exchanged a few words.

"Well," Nicolas returned to the brothers. "That's all the stuff they have. Let's go." He took a box from the cart and set off. But Jeremiah stopped him with a question.

"Wait a minute, Nicolas. Can you ask him some questions?"

Nicolas put the box on the floor. "Sure."

"Ask him how long he's worked at City Hall." Another brief exchange in Polish.

"Twenty-seven years."

Jeremiah was impressed.

"It's a long time. Was he born here?"

Nicolas translated, and this time Hans responded with one word short, fast, and less cheerful. Jeremiah did not need translation this time.

"Ask him... ask him if there were ever any Jews living round here."

Nicolas translated, and the smile completely disappeared from Hans's face. This startling question was certainly unexpected. Suddenly he remembered his father, and what he always said about... Jews. He studied the bearded man in front of him, and suddenly the bill in his pocket began to weigh heavy, very heavy. Had he made a mistake with these documents? Suddenly today did not seem quite so bright.

"No. He says no Jews ever lived round here."

"Even before the war? Even then?"

Nicolas's words jarred Hans's ears. The documents they requested... they were from a dark period in local history. He looked at the boxes, which were stacked near the exit. Could he ask for them back? The Jewish money burned in his pocket. He knew he could still return it. It was not too late. He could still return the document boxes to the same place they had lain for years. But bottles of vodka (yes, he decided, it's better to forget than to savor) winked at him, and payday was far away, too far. It wasn't every day he landed such a huge sum, and who knows? Maybe there was more where that came from. They looked like they were going to need his services in the future. And he would be there, he decided. He would be there to serve them...and keep an eye on them.

Nicolas repeated his question, and Hans replied with clerical confidence, and flavored his answer in a phrase that made Nicolas blush, given the holy clerics standing next to him. Not everything needs to be translated, Nicolas thought as he listened to Hans' cold laughter, and in English he said Jews never lived there.

*

Less than an hour later Nicolas was buried deep beneath a mountain of documents from the first box, which covered the two beds stacked up high. Jeremiah and Isaiah stood to the side, a little helpless, watching Nicolas continue to pull out more and more old papers from the carton.

"So..." began Jeremiah, "that's all about this town before the Soviet regime?"

"What survived the war, yes."

"It's a lot of material and only you can read it."

"Yes... and it's not even in order. I must actually examine every document."

Jeremiah looked over the stack of papers on his bed and the four larger boxes next to it. Yes, it was going to take a very long time

"Okay," said Isaiah. "Let's think for a moment. We're looking for information about a pair of twins born sometime during the war."

"Or twin birth certificates, death certificates, certificates of adoption... everything can be important. Overall, there was a war here and much disorder. The Nazis retreated to Germany, the Russians and the Americans walked around here..."

"Yes. Certificates of birth or death of twins," Nicolas agreed.

"And whatever can attest to Jews who lived here."

"... Or Christians," said Isaiah.

Their eyes wandered again over the boxes. Yes, it would take a very long time. Days, for sure. Maybe a week. And in the meantime?

"Do you want to take a walk around?" asked Isaiah. And they turned to leave.

*

Nabradosky's streets were a little brighter this afternoon, although it was impossible to suspect them of being over-friendly. Still, it was more pleasant to drive, and the forests surrounding the town, so the brothers decided, were even more pleasant. They had another reason to visit there.

"Let's go to where White said he found us."

"In the war?"

*

The sound of helicopters landing had long since ceased to disturb Eva's daily routine. That is what happened, it turned out, when you lived on a military base long enough. You got used to the rotor noise, started to yell (naturally) as a helicopter approached, stopped talking when it was right overhead, and continued in the same way (naturally) until it had passed by.

Military life. A life filled with cutting sounds, burning scents, sharp colors. This was the life Eva had chosen, and she got used to every sight and sound of it.

Except for this one sound.

She squeezed the trigger, and made it again.

*

It turned out that the she was lacking some hours on the shooting range. She had not held a weapon in a serious manner for several weeks, since she left the United States for Germany. And now she had finally got a booking at the shooting range, she savored every bullet.

A light squeeze on the trigger... and a familiar shiver went through her bones, her shoulders and down her spine. She created another hole in the human figure, exactly 30 feet away, slightly below and to the right of the painted shoulder. Yes, pure pleasure.

Next to her were more soldiers, each in his own lane, with his own target. Yes, that was another thing that she loved about the shooting range - complete seclusion in a private world, in a private fight, you against yourself. She was vaguely aware that Miguel stood at the next lane. Like her, he waged his own private war.

Another shot. Another tick. Another hole in the paper target, this time closer to the ear of the target...

And hers.

She heard a bullet whizz by her ear, buzzing angrily. Something in her heart shifted. She squeezed the trigger again, and a sharp pain seared the edge of her right thigh. Something snapped at her face... and her nostrils breathed a different air from the firing range air.

The air burned her lungs. Trees galloped ahead, and her back screamed in pain. There was another rifle barking behind her-

The sharp scent of gunpowder disrupted her sense of direction, or maybe there was some other reason for it? Eva did not know, but her next bullet did not hit the form in front of her at all. Nor did the next one. Her vision swam and the paper figure took a life of its own, ducked, dodged-

Around the corner, with death close behind her, she felt some relief. The barking gun now sounded a little distant, and bullets were no longer buzzing around her ears. Maybe she'd lost him? She looked down at the twins' crib. She smiled at them.

The target stabilized in front of her again, and Eva wiped away her sweat, trying to concentrate, squeezing the trigger - and a hole punctured the paper, but not the target that once again eluded her to

89

the right. She squeezed off another two quick shots, both of which missed their target's head, which continued to dance in front of her, dodging and bending. Was it just her imagination playing tricks with her? She felt herself sinking, drowning in greenish, cool fog.

Trees in front of her swirled into a unified green hell of leaves, twigs and moss on wet rocks. Her breathing became short, and the pain from her leg wound became more tangible. She went on and slowed down, went on and failed. Death was close behind her, walking toward her with an easy stride. She felt a gun sight zooming on the back of her neck. She was being watched from behind. Determined, her finger squeezed the trigger – but instead of a shot, there was a clatter.

The weapon ran out of ammunition.

Yet she was no longer conscious to know that.

*

At the same time, a few hundred miles away, the two brothers breathed cool and green air. Sweet pine scent sharpened their consciousness, and without knowing why, the two brothers were able to breathe deeper, calmer.

From the moment they emerged from the bowels of the town, they were relaxed and happier. Their neck muscles relaxed as did their shoulders, which had been tense for a few days now. They returned to nature. Maybe it was the nature which eased their minds, replacing the grey concrete with wooded green. Maybe it was something else.

The paved road diverged into a number of muddy paths.

"Turn here."

And Isaiah turned. They were about three kilometers east of the village, in a heavily forested area of dense green conifers. The path narrowed into the deep green, winding between dense, tall and thick trees.

Suddenly Isaiah stamped on the brakes. The jeep slid a few feet forward, and Jeremiah saw the reason for the sudden halt.

Just before the next curve in the road, less than fifty meters ahead, was parked Jerric's green truck.

The brothers looked at it in silence then, as one, emerged from their vehicle. Without a word they advanced toward the green truck, then turned right and disappeared into the trees. At a little distance in front of them, they heard murmurs and then a dry cough.

Little by little the coughing began to expose Jerric's whereabouts within the tangle of trees and foliage. Finally, the twins came up behind a large tree which gave them a broad point of view over the clearing ahead.

It was not a big clearing, a few feet from one side to the other bank, barely containing a small heap, well-padded with green moss. A man just passing through the forest would probably not even look at it twice. But Jerric, who was wearing a black coat, looked at it intently, muttering in an unknown language.

"You understand any of it?" whispered Isaiah.

Jeremiah shook his head. "It doesn't sound like Polish."

Jerric's murmuring was cut short as he broke out in a fit of tough, sharp coughs again, that unlike its predecessor, did not pass so quickly. On the contrary. The longer the coughing went on, the worse it got and along with the guttural hacking, he started to gasp for air. Jerric staggered and sat down on the ground, holding his chest.

"I have to check it out."

Before Jeremiah could react, Isaiah was out of whispering range. Reluctantly, he stood up, brushed a little mud off his pants and hurried to catch up with his brother.

Jerric, still spasmodically coughing, saw the two brothers approaching. He took a deep breath and managed to calm the cough a bit.

"I thought you'd left already," he wheezed. His coughing erupted again, lasting several minutes. Isaiah patted his back lightly to ease the cough.

"We wanted to look around a little more," he said. "Good air here... are you okay?"

Jerric waved his hand dismissively, and spat from the back of his throat.

"You are not safe here. I already told you."

The brothers looked at each other. All trace of the temporary relief in their mood was long gone. Jerric, sitting on the damp ground in front of them, now seemed old and sick, yet dark and threatening far beyond his physical capability. There was something in him that made them want to run and run... but they had a goal and they were going to get it.

"We need to find out some more details, see some documents."

Jerric nodded almost imperceptibly. He tried to get up, but gave up on his first attempt. Jeremiah, who until now had been quiet, offered him his hand and pulled him up from the ground. He looked at the mound of old stones carefully.

"What brings you here?"

Jerric also looked at the low mound and his eyes lost focus. Jeremiah thought he was going to collapse again, but then Jerric regained his balance and answered quietly.

"Memories."

"May I ask of what?"

"It's of no interest to you youngsters. These are old memories..."

"We're looking for old memories."

"But not like this, not like that."

The wind, which was imperceptible until that moment, grew stronger around them and whistled though the green foliage. Loud, lonely silence wrapped around them. Jerric looked at them softly, sadly, arousing something familiar in the heart of the priest. He knew that look. Maybe too well."

"I noticed that there isn't a church here. If you want, I can..."

Jerric launched into a mirthless chuckle. Nabradosky did not have a church, although in recent years, he knew more and more people had begun to turn to the warm bosom of Christianity. But Jerric, he never thought of going to church, and was certainly not about to start today. So he shook his head, coughed twice and leaned against a tree nearby.

"No confessions. Not for me."

Jeremiah and Isaiah exchanged glances, and one of them was about to speak, but Jerric beat him to it with a closing comment of some finality.

"Now, if you'll excuse me, let an old man be alone with his memories… please."

*

Their journey back to the hotel was quiet and thoughtful. Isaiah was busy driving, Jeremiah looked past the trees and both ran it over and over in their minds, this profound meeting with Jerric. There was, in this man, something a little supernatural, something a little unreal. They knew, they felt, that somewhere in their past, they knew him. They knew it, they felt it, but both refused to accept their feelings.

"I don't believe a word he said," Jeremiah finally said.

"You judge people too quickly. Seems to me he is actually very old, very tired..."

"Very deceitful."

"... very sad," Isaiah finished his sentence.

Jeremiah looked at him and could not agree. Jerric really looked sad and tired. Isaiah considered. *Jeremiah was right*, he thought. *The man blatantly lied to them.*

The path climbed back to the paved road, and the conversation came back to life. They talked about Jerric and the forest and that low, mossy rubble mound and tall trees. By the time they got back to the grey town they were already in a heated discussion on the chances that Jews had lived there in town. Street followed street, turn chased turn, and when the two-story tavern stood before them once more, they had found solidarity in furiously attacking the fact that there was not even one church in Nabradosky.

"A few years of communism and people lose all connection to God." Isaiah was panting up the stairs and went into the hallway on the second floor. Two doors on both sides of the hall were open and Kristzah, the maid, was dusting in the left room. Isaiah gave her no more than a passing glance. He was busy with more important things.

"No wonder this regime has fallen... it just had no soul - "

And suddenly he felt he was talking to an empty space. He looked back to see Jeremiah standing, fascinated, a few steps behind him. His face was expressionless and his eyes were glazed, entirely mesmerized some point before him.

"Jeremiah?"

And his brother began to walk, slowly, into the room. With no idea of what captivated him, Isaiah frowned and went back, looking at Jeremiah's retreating back. Then he saw the two things that had caught his brother's interest. Saw them, and shuddered.

93

An old memory washed over the brothers. An old picture, a moment in time, buried for years under an avalanche of other fresher moments. The old wound hurt the brothers with a pain they had not felt for many years – the sweet pain of a mental scab peeled off an old memory, etched deep in the complexities of the brain, coming into the world fifty years after being buried for good.

And in the memory was a young woman, the same young woman, raising her hands in front of two silver candlesticks, the slim, shining light of two twinkling candles. The woman's eyes were closed, she wore a scarf on her head, and was muttering something to herself, something to her children...

*

"Shabbase."

Kristzah's strident voice drew the brothers out of their dreams. They turned in a slight panic, torn by the sweet sadness of the memory. Kristzah smiled a toothless smile at them, a feather duster in one hand, her other hand pointing to the candlesticks.

"Shabbase," she repeated and explained, as if to put some intelligence back into the brothers.

Jeremiah was overwhelmed.

*

Two minutes later they had fetched Nicolas and were all inside the room with the door closed behind them and Kristzah was sitting on the bed. The old woman did not understand completely what the commotion was about, but she liked it – it was many years since anyone had taken so much interest in her. Almost all her life, actually.

And Jeremiah was as interested in her as he had been interested in anything for many years. He was all excited and stressed, he talked to Nicolas at a rate of a machine gun, speaking in fragments between inhaling and exhaling.

"I want to know where those candlesticks came from, how did she get them, how did she know that these are Shabbat candlesticks..."

"They do not have to be for Shabbat..." Isaiah was able to sneak a word in.

94

"... And how does she even know what Shabbat is, and in Yiddish! Shabbase!"

The flow of questions left Nicolas slightly at a loss. He started asking Kristzah something right at the beginning of Jeremiah's words, but immediately mixed the questions, and he did not know where to start. Isaiah, the calmest of the three, imposed order in the situation.

"Let's start at the beginning. Where she was born, what she remembers from the war..."

Nicolas listened, paused for a second, and then asked in Polish, "Tell us, Nana, how old were you at the time of the war?"

Kristzah, smiling until now, stopped smiling. She opened her toothless mouth, and began to speak from the depths of memory. She told them...

*

... She told them her first memory, the colors and shapes as early as she could remember, when she was still a little girl in a small village. She tried to tell them what happened before the first memory, and was sure that there was indeed something...but she could not remember. Too many years, too many fires.

So she told them. She told them about the little girl, a ghostly girl, six or seven years old, playing in a field near the village, chasing butterflies. It was a white butterfly with brown eyes that slipped from her grasp over and over again, until finally it escaped into the trees, leaving behind the bright world of green. A cloud of dust rose from a big car on the dirt road.

The little girl went between the trees, looking for the butterfly. She did not find it, but instead she spotted a cute squirrel looking down at her and skipped between the trees to chase it. She followed, humming and happy, careless of time and away from her chores. Her whole life was ahead of her, she knew, and the laundry she carried waited for her, too, she knew, but now it was just her and the squirrel, just her and her sweet happiness -

Boom boom, Ta-Ta-Ta-Ta-Ta-Ta-Ta - Boom Boom Ta-Ta-Ta-Ta-Ta - Boom Ta-Ta-Ta —

High, sharp sounds pierced the forest. Shots.

95

She awoke from her own thoughts. She stopped humming. The sounds went on and on cracking the silence of the forest without mercy, without distinction. The ghostly girl in the white dress suddenly wanted to go home, and fast.

She turned back… but the path was long gone and all around her was just the forest, tall, thick and menacing. She had already whiled away many hours in the woods around the house, but always knew how to get out of them. But this time?

This time she knew nothing: not direction, nor distance.

A small tear appeared at the corner of her eye and a little thought whispered to her that she would never find her way home. She would never see her mother and father again, she would never play with the neighbor's children. This thought grew and grew, filling her chest with fear and the white ghostly girl started to cry softly, then loudly.

She knew she was to blame. She dropped the laundry and ran into the woods, and now God would punish her, and harshly. She wanted to go home so much. In her heart she promised and vowed never would she run off again, never would she leave her parents alone, never laugh, never-

And she knew it was too late. She had lost her home, her world and would never return to them again.

She wandered among the trees, a small white figure among the green giants, bumping the lower branches, sinking into the mountains of fallen leaves. She had never been to this part of the forest, so she never learned the way out.

The noise of vehicles came from her right, a heavy, crawling noise. She started to run toward it, and after two minutes she broke out of the woods and into the dimming light outside. A long line of military vehicles passed by - tanks and jeeps carrying grownups, tired but happy with life.

One of the vehicles stopped next to her and someone inside spoke to her. Again she felt that something was wrong... this was not a language that she had heard before. He spoke to her again, and again, and finally she did the natural thing, the first thing small children when they do not understand: she burst into tears.

It worked.

Strong hands lifted her into the vehicle, wrapping her in a woolen blanket and giving her a drink of water from a warm canteen. The vehicle started forward again and although it was not really comfortable, she found herself falling asleep in the warmth of the blanket, surrounded by monotonous and soothing engine noise.

*

She woke up when the engine stopped.
Her village! Home!
But not exactly.
It looked like her village, similar, but not exactly her village. The houses looked like the same houses, but other people lived in them. True, some of the faces remained the same, but not exactly the same. Another part was completely different, and the gazes - oh, the gazes! - the gazes were different. Not peaceful, nor happy, but strained and empty.

It was not her village. It was just *like* it. As if her parents were gone, or, rather, *changed*. Her father was replaced by another father, and her mother refused to look at her or talk to her, as if she did not recognize her.

She tried to hug her, but was rejected. She ran to someone that looked like their neighbor - and was received coldly. They did not know her, did not know who she was. They did not want her there. And she, suddenly, did not want to stay there. She did not want the strange new world. This was so similar but very different from the world which she came from.

But it, sighed Kristzah, was her punishment for shirking the laundry and chasing after butterflies into the forest.

Eventually, she went on, she stayed in the new village and grew up alongside those who were similar to her neighbors. She did not remember much of what happened after, in her childhood. Everything got mixed up for her, a swirling frenziedly in a painfully familiar world, and strange to a point of constant terror, with no relatives and without her parents.

She never stopped hoping that one day she would return to them.

After she finished speaking, Kristzah sat still on the chair and sobbed out the rest of her inner pain. The two brothers were quiet and other than a comforting hand that the priest laid on her, they could do nothing. Jeremiah suspected, quite rightly, that this was the first time she had told her story, not only to others, but also to herself.

Finally she ran out of tears. She left behind the girl she once was, and came back to the reality of the here and now. Her eyes dried up and a sense of shame flashed through them, as if she was naked. She wrapped her arms around her, hugging the old body that had become hers over the years. With polite, shy apologies to Nicolas, she muttered a few words, and left the room.

The brothers watched her go then, looked at Nicolas.

"Poor woman."

The brothers agreed, and Jeremiah asked about the candlesticks.

"These aren't her candlesticks," recalled Nicolas, as if he had completely forgotten why Kristzah began to tell her story in the first place. "She doesn't know where they're from. She didn't know what Shabbase is - just that they are called that."

*

Night descended upon Europe.

Eva Neumann, formal in her doctors' uniform, continued her efforts to clear her mind from everything that had happened today. Fortunately, routine work in the clinic helped her with that. A stable and thinning influx of soldiers with minor problems continued to fill the waiting room, asking for headache pills, creams for jock itches, and in the case of an urgent and difficult case (and the last) sitting in front of her: elastic bandage.

"You're not going to war this week," she patted the soldier's injured knee. "And no basketball."

The results of the 'terrible' news were evident on the face of the young soldier. Shock, grief, disappointment... Eva almost laughed.

"Okay," he blurted out, and Eva sent him to someone to bandage his leg properly.

"... And Irene, if there's no one else out there, you're dismissed. I'll tidy up here."

Irene nodded, but Eva did not see it. Weighed down with heavy thoughts again, she moved to the larger part of the clinic, not usually open to soldiers with simple complaints.

This, in fact, was a modern emergency room and totally sophisticated, including a sterile operating room at the end, which could be ready for emergency operations within five minutes. Eva remembered how surprised she was when she saw it for the first time, not long ago, and how she detected the most important element in a large American military base soldiers: quiet, soft beds, away from noise.

With a sigh, she lay down on one of them, stretched out, closed her eyes and began to massage her temples lightly. She slowly began to return to her last day's events, including (and especially... especially!) that frightening experience at the shooting range, where she met for the first time in daylight, her old childhood dream.

Yes, she realized suddenly. This was not the first time she had run through those trees with shots after her. Her skin crawled and her nipples perked up. A cold shock crawled up her spine, making its way to her consciousness. No, she realized, it was not the first time that the experience was so realistic, it was not the first time she ran for her life, fled for her life and... whose life? Who were they, those she was trying to save?

"It's about time you took a rest," she heard a familiar voice.

Suddenly she opened her eyes to reality.

He was so handsome. Miguel stood beside her, a charming smile on his face, and just a pinch of concern hidden in his eyes. *I scared him*, she knew. But he knew how to do the right thing. Knew how to be with her. For her. And now he stroked her cheek as well.

"What, just what would I do without you?"

"By now? Care for four small Jewish children, most likely..."

She laughed very loudly, very liberating.

"Probably..." she blurted out between one broken breath and the other. Miguel had a very fine sense of humor and often teased her choices as the elder daughter of a senior rabbi in New York. This time the humor was in place, very much in place.

He continued to stroke her cheek.

"You scared us at the shooting range. Like you'd seen a ghost or something."

The laughter died, and made room for a vague smile.

"Yeah... I know. Sorry. It was... I was suddenly very cold, and I was scared..." Then it struck her. New news, cold and very solid: "I dreamed I saw my father, Miguel."

Miguel chuckled.

"Luckily, your father's in New York, Evie."

Eva was completely serious. "No, he's actually in Poland."

"Poland?"

"Yes, my mother told me... he and his brother went on some roots trip."

"The priest brother?" If there was one thing Miguel loved in the story of Jeremiah and his brother, it was the irony of it. Miguel was a Catholic, and he really wanted to meet the Christian uncle that suddenly landed in the Orthodox family of his future wife. *Maybe now there will be a better chance...*

"Yes. The priest."

Miguel looked at Eva's worried eyes, feeling very self-reflective. Jeremiah's very close proximity bothered him in a way he did not fully understand. Not without surprise, he found he was actually happy about their distance from the United States. He was pleased that an ocean separated his love and her... oppressive family.

Now, with Eva's rabbinical father running around Poland, less than two hours' flight away, he felt that was much worse. *Roots campaign*, he thought. *I wonder what they expect to find.*

*

They found their first significant clue to the history of Nabradosky the next morning, less than five minutes away from their room.

That Friday morning was wet and muddy after a night of constant trickle from the sky. Unlike the Soviet parts of the town which were paved with broken concrete and steel, the old part of Nabradosky grew directly out of the ground without a hint of asphalt or pavement.

The paths between the houses had become a batter of black mud, laid with cold and muddy puddles.

Even on a clear day, Jeremiah admitted to himself, this was not one of the most beautiful places in the world, let alone in such bad weather. The three large trees, by which the brothers identified the town, still stood in the center of the neighborhood. Scattered around them were some small white cabins in various states of repair, some no more than a crumbling ruins, missing the roof. The "streets" were defined by strips of mud and some gravel. Vegetation, wild and uncultivated, invaded them from the yards of the houses.

Movement in this part of the town consisted of a skinny cow and some chickens which scattered plaintively when the brothers' Lada came along. Other than that, not even a single man was seen in the street, not a soul among the houses.

They parked near the three trees and slipped out of it in a mournful silence. They tightened their coats and looked around at their surroundings. As the weather slightly improved the rain subsided to a slow, prickly trickle, which gently encouraged the brothers close to the tree trunks under protective foliage.

With their backs to the trunks they took a look at the gloomy town, trying to think where to start, still without a word exchanged between them, not one word, not even a glance. Cold, heavy feelings moved through their bodies, drying their mouths, wrinkling their frowning foreheads. The cold rain sprinkled around them and only the trees' needles prevented them from dripping with it.

Without realizing it, Isaiah stroked the third tree's dead bark with his hand. It felt cold, rough and dry. No new growth, no sap. It was only a dry shell, slightly weathered by time. But, one thing was strange about it. Isaiah felt it slightly with his fingers, wondering what it meant, then turned to his brother.

"Look at this, Jeremiah."

The dead trunk was full of bullet holes. Not one, but many. Not masked, as were the two other trees (and as they discovered after seconds) but visible. In their depths, some metallic, dull rust shimmered.

Jeremiah recalled his old dream.

101

In the dream, he was in this same environment, terrifyingly familiar. But he was not in the same recurring dream that he had experienced countless times. It was a duller dream, more broken. But it had (yes, it had... it had!) three large trees... and shots rang out... and bullets whistled by... and people were running and falling.

And a certain man ran in front of these trees and fell... and fell...

*

Jeremiah's gaze wandered to the next house. "Let's go."

The rain did not change its rhythm and cold drops penetrated the gap between the collar of Isaiah's thin coat and his neck. Jeremiah was protected by the black hat, and for the first time in Poland, he felt a little at home. After all, his attire, he knew, was traditional Eastern European. It was designed for this weather, grim as it may be.

They continued to explore the abandoned houses, looking right and left. Not all the houses were deserted: some were painted and maintained, with relatively new wooden doors. New - and locked. More cows were tied to a tree sticking up from the ground, piles of wet feed nearby.

The landscape was so similar to that in Jeremiah's dream... but, certainly, it was the view from the hundreds of small towns in Poland and possibly Russia. Tiny towns, godforsaken, abandoned in another time, another era.

For several minutes they wandered among the houses, accompanied by the sound of the thin trickle of rain. Puddle spilled into puddle, an uncultivated yard blended into the indefinite street. In America, Jeremiah thought to himself, you would find shacks and cardboard boxes in such an area. Here things were a little different.

He turned his attention to Isaiah, who wandered by. Like him, he was silent, his brow furrowed, his eyes distant. Jeremiah knew why.

"Isaiah, do you have dreams?"

"Dreams - you mean, daydreaming?"

"No. I mean a real dreams."

Isaiah sighed. Dreams were his specialty from back in his school days. He was daydreaming his days away in daydreams and waking up at night to sweat-soaked beds. This time, he knew exactly what his twin meant. And his heart contracted.

"I have one of these... recurring dreams. In a town like this. Only this one... it doesn't look like a dream. More like a distant memory."

"Memory of what?"

"Well, there are two babies in a basket. I mean I think they are both babies. Because I used to be a baby, and beside me..."

"... Another baby. In a wicker basket."

They looked at each other, a mysterious light in their eyes. They both knew, suddenly, that they had shared the same dream for years, the same, and it was an amazing feeling - that only identical twins can share. It was a great joy, exciting... but there was also the other part, the dark part of that dream.

"And there's our mother. She takes us in her hands, and runs with us."

"Mom... yes. She's afraid of something."

"She's scared, yes. Scared to death."

Isaiah stopped. New feelings crept up his throat, remembering something he thought dead and buried long ago. He returned at once to a distant childhood, to cold nights under a thick blanket.

"I remember... when I was little, I would crawl into bed with mom and dad at night. They were hugging me. Relaxing me. Yeah... every time it happened, Dad would open the Psalm book and read to me. By the age of five I knew the book by heart."

The rain stopped, and the light drizzle disappeared from the empty streets. They continued to walk through muddy puddles not knowing what they were looking for, not sure they wanted to find it. Alley after alley, house after house, the doors remained locked. Sounds of gravel trampled under their shoes were the only sounds they heard.

"Where is everybody?" Jeremiah wondered. "It's two in the afternoon, the middle of the day..."

Jeremiah could not understand it. After some thought, he brought his two hands to his mouth, like a speaker, shouting with a loud and strong voice, "Hello!! Is anyone there?"

Only a faint echo answered.

103

But behind them came another sound. A door opened, creaking slightly on its hinges, and they turned with a smile. But it died as soon as they saw the little boy come out of it, and a maternal hand drew him back in. The door closed, locked and the small window next to it was pulled shut.

They looked at each other. That was an overreaction. They went up and knocked the door.

"Hello?" demanded Isaiah.

A few seconds of silence passed, while they listened for any whispering inside. Isaiah was about to knock again, but at that moment the door opened. Not wide, but through the narrow slit they could see the face of an older woman, aged about fifty. She looked at them with a frozen face and her white fingers clenched the handle.

Nicolas was not with them so Isaiah recruited the little Polish he had picked up along the way and stuttered, "Hello, I - "

But the Polish woman decided she had heard enough. Aloud, she said, "No, no, no, no," and slammed the door in their faces. The lock was turned again.

Isaiah moved away from the door. "What is it with these people?" he said almost angrily, turning to walk a few steps toward the street.

But then he saw that his brother was not with him. Instead, Jeremiah remained at the locked door, examining something on the doorpost. He approached him.

"Isaiah, look at this."

Other than a sunken angled niche in the stone doorpost, Isaiah had not noticed anything unusual.

"This was the house of Jewish people."

Jeremiah's voice was cold, dry and emotionless. And yet, something began to vibrate in him.

"Home of Jewish... how d'you get to that?"

A long Jewish finger reached out, stroking the carved stone niche. "Mezuzah."

Isaiah's pupils widened. He knew what a mezuzah was. How did that verse go...? Yes: *"You shall write them on the doorframes of your houses and on your gates "*...

"This is a mezuzah," continued his brother. "A place to put the holy verses. You have it at the entrance of every Jewish home..." His

104

voice trailed off and he slowly withdrew behind his frown. He removed himself from the doorway, and walked quickly to the house next door, Isaiah trailing behind him. It also had that naked niche, a silent, lonely witness to the distant past of those houses. An involuntary tremor whipped his shoulders.

"Here too," he said and knocked on the door. No one answered. He knocked again, this time, harder. The house was closed, and although it was not well-maintained there were clear signs of life. The knocking turned into fist blows that rocked the door loudly.

Jeremiah kicked the door once, then backed away, upset. A tear of sweat formed on his forehead.

"Why won't anyone open up?" he asked the empty street aloud.

Something began to burn in his bones, to energize his legs. A loud buzzing sounded in his ears and his vision began to redden and shake from side to side. He ran to the edge of the street, and stopped at another house that caught his attention.

Unlike the two other houses, this was a real dump, no door, no roof, no interior furnishings. In the gloomy light that swept the street, he recognized that Mezuzah niche in the door-post, and his heart sped full-gallop.

Jeremiah took a deep breath and stepped inside. The stone floor was well padded with rough weeds, greenery having claimed ownership of the house. But between the tiles and on the walls more color could be seen, not a natural one. Jeremiah ran his finger over the wall and looked closely.

Coal.

Jeremiah wandered inside, looked round. The cottage had three rooms, all with sooty walls. He looked at the posts of the interior doors. He nodded his head sadly.

"This... this is a Mezuzah... Mezuzah... Mezuzah... and this... this was certainly a Jewish home."

A tear began to take shape at the corner of his eye, a little hint of the storm that broke out inside his heart. A storm that destroys, eats and screams. He ran outside, tears in his eyes.

"*Houses of Jews...*" he muttered to himself, as if he did not believe his words.

Then: "*Murderers!*"

105

The harsh statement soared along the empty street penetrating locked doors. Small children, who were not allowed to go out, skipped a beat. Mothers, fearing the worst, rechecked the door bolts. And the rain, oh the rain came back even stronger.

"*Murderers!*" he called again, directing blame at the locked houses.

He splashed through puddles, looking for a living soul, looking for something to hit, to take revenge on. A hand grabbed him from behind, and he almost responded to it with violence. But it was Isaiah. He abruptly shook him off and moved on, crying, screaming.

Isaiah grabbed him again, trying to hold him, but Jeremiah shook him off again wildly. His eyes were red and swollen. A vein in his forehead pulsed strongly.

"Jeremiah, stop..."

But Jeremiah did not stop. He crossed over the road and looked at the doorpost of another house, where he found another mezuzah. He looked at his brother with an accusing glare.

"Look. Look! They took our homes. Shamelessly!" He clenched his fist and began to pound the door, shaking it. "Come out," he pounded. "I - want - to - talk –to - you!"

But though no door opened, not a shutter was raised, although no one made a sound, the rain filled it all with white noise, flooding it, and Jeremiah moved to the middle of the street, stunned.

"*One of these houses was our home. Ours! With our mother! And our father!*"

And there he stopped and burst into tears. Isaiah came closer to him again, gathered him up and hugged him in his arms. This time Jeremiah did not reject it, but simply stood there, sobbing, shaking in hot waves, blazing, with the rain dripping around them.

"*Look what they did to us! Those... those Christians of yours! Murdered them all... burned them all, murdered...*"

His voice trailed off and stopped. Absorbed by the strong embrace of his twin brother, the spasms in his body stopped and he could breathe regularly again.

An intense sound of shattering glass broke the moment.

They sprang apart, a new look of alarm in their eyes.

"*The car...*" Isaiah said, and began to move toward large trees.

Another smashing sound made them both start running, shouting, "Hey! Hey!" It took less than a minute to go around the corner, but it was not fast enough. Their jeep was still there, but its every window was shattered.

And on the hood was a swastika scratched in the paint.

*

They remotely heard a sound of someone running away, but only managed to see his back as he ran away, and his shaved head.

Lies

"He that worketh deceit shall not dwell within my house; He that speaketh falsehood shall not be established before mine eyes." (Psalms 101:7)

The broken windows made the journey back much wetter and colder, growing worse as the minutes passed. The dubious pleasure of sitting on broken glass did not add much to the experience, although before getting in they cleared most of the debris off the seats. The pouring rain made this task quite dangerous, indeed, Jeremiah cut his hand on a particularly elusive piece.

Finally they set out, still dazed.

While Isaiah drove in silence, Jeremiah took the opportunity to talk with Hannah on his cellphone. The connection was surprisingly lucid and clear, despite the increased wind noise. Hannah answered after several rings, and Jeremiah tried to sound as ordinary as he could.

"Alright, Hannah. A bit boring."

Isaiah listened in on the call and his thoughts wandered. He recognized the cozy softness Jeremiah plunged into, the softness of that family unit that he, himself, did not know very well. He remembered Hannah well from the few meetings between them. He remembered her luminous strength, the way she calmed the storms around them. Yes, he could fall in love with her, he decided. Happily, his brother had chosen her.

"No, don't worry. Make sure the girls study. Look after Rachel, okay? We can't let it happen to her... like what happened to her... sister. She's staying at Beit Yaacov and that's the end of that story!"

Isaiah nodded to himself. He knew a little about the rift between Jeremiah and his daughter. His keen senses told him that Hannah was trying to recruit him to soften his brother's rigid stance. *And really, why accept his twin brother as a Christian, but not accept a Christian husband for his eldest daughter? There was a certain injustice... though he certainly understood his brother. Would I let my daughter marry a Jew, not a good Catholic?* He did not like the answer he gave himself.

"Jews? Found something about it, but I can't talk about it on the phone... no, we don't need help, we found what we were looking for... we'll be back after the Sabbath. Uh..."

Maybe it was Isaiah's perceptive gaze, maybe it was remembering too late who was sitting beside him, but something caused Jeremiah to hesitate a little, and correct himself.

"... After Sunday, I mean... okay, I'll call you later."

110

Jeremiah turned off the phone and Isaiah wasted not a second.

"What do you mean, we found what we were looking for? I don't think so!"

"You don't? The Jewish houses? Houses destroyed? What more do you want? A written confession?"

"You only say that because you're convinced in advance that you're right. Perhaps Christians also lived here? Maybe it wasn't here, like Jerric said?"

Jeremiah snorted contemptuously.

"Jerric? That old man looked us in the eye and lied to us! He's hiding something from us."

"Maybe, maybe not."

The rest of the road passed in determined silence. Isaiah felt that somehow he had hurt his brother, but could not help putting the other side of the argument. There was only one way Jeremiah could see reality, only one interpretation of what they found. True, Jerric was probably hiding something, but it seemed he hid it in their favor. And true - the doorposts of the houses probably indicated that there were once Jews there. So what? It did not mean they were their parents!

Isaiah could not help but feel a little frustrated.

*

His frustration grew as soon as they entered their room, still in silence. Nicolas sat on the bed, in the center of a storm scattered documents. When he looked up, the look in his eyes ranged from despair to boredom.

"Well, is there anything?"

Nicolas shrugged. The documents on the bed, numerous as they were, represented only a small part of what still waited for them in the boxes. Already Nicolas seemed lost among the massive amounts of worthless, unfocused, meaningless data.

"Not yet," he said. "But I've just started."

There was a knock at the door, and before any of them could react, it opened. Kristzah hurried inside with a tray in her hand. She closed

111

the door behind her and locked it. Jeremiah and Isaiah, still standing, exchanged glances.

"Everything okay, Kristzah?" asked Nicolas in Polish.

"Yes, yes. I brought you food. You must be hungry."

Nicolas smiled. "Thank you, but why? We can eat downstairs - with everyone."

The old woman's agitated response almost startled them. Kristzah began to shake her head wildly, choked up, and urgently whispered unclear words. Nicolas rushed to silence her, and finally she calmed down.

"No, no! Don't go down," she blurted out between breaths and whispered, "They talk about you... not good talk."

Jeremiah did not understand this little scene enacted before him in dramatic Polish. He touched Nicolas's shoulder.

"What does she want, Nicolas?"

"She brought us food, so we won't go downstairs. Seems that... people are talking about us there."

Isaiah frowned, opened the door and peered out into the hall. No one was there. Jeremiah watched his movements, and then continued to ask, "Talk? Ask her who's talking."

"Who's talking about us there, Kristzah?"

Her response was no more understandable than the documents on the bed.

"They are. They are!"

"They? Who are they?" Nicolas asked loudly, almost shouting.

But Kristzah immediately pressed her hand to his mouth.

"Shhhh.... do not mention them. They are not like us. Do not mention them. It's bad. Very bad to mention them. Very bad."

Then, as if she had suddenly become aware of her bizarre behavior, she released Nicolas's gagged mouth and giggled a nervous laugh, half insane, certainly on the brink. She put her hand over her own mouth this time, and without saying anything else, went out of the room.

Who's talking about us, Jeremiah thought. *And where?*

*

It was the five old people who sat in a large, elegant room, only minutes' drive away from them.

The large room was hidden in the basement of the most luxurious house in Nabradosky. The surrounding brick wall, the large and beautiful yard, the electric security gate and other luxuries separated this property from those of the ordinary people.

The symbols of prestige continued into the house and the basement room was no exception. It was entirely paneled in wood, lined with expensive Uzbek carpets and furnished with black leather sofas. In the center of the room stood a heavy wooden table embellished with ornate French engravings.

On the table were five cups, hot marble cake and two bottles of imported cognac.

On the sofas were five respectable-looking people: Jerric, well-dressed as usual, and next to him Erich, Franz, Thomas and Andzej, all of whom Jeremiah and Isaiah had seen that first night they spent in Nabradosky. But something had changed in them since that evening in the tavern. Now they were more solemn. Almost concerned.

"It's been a long time since we last met like this," opened Jerric.

The others nodded. Years had passed since they had all been in the same room, and no one thought they would ever need to do it again.

"The... these tourists," said Erich. "They're causing problems."

He pointed to Franz, who was sitting next to him, who continued by explaining hoarsely, "They visited the old village today. Entered the old buildings."

"Yes?" asked Jerric. "What did they say?"

Franz shook his head. He did not understand English, and Jerric knew it, but it was not the reason that he did not know what the tourists had said.

"Erich's grandson is the one who saw them."

Jerric turned his blue eyes to Erich, and Erich shivered slightly. He did not like those eyes, did not like the fact that his grandson got mixed up in this conversation. There are things you must do alone, without family, without grandchildren. It was not their business, and Franz did not have to mention him. Jerric was still waiting.

"Yes... hmm... he saw them poking around. I don't like it, Jerric."

Eyes continued to look at him coldly. Erich hated them, the way they poked holes in him. He hated Jerric - he realized that a long time ago, but there was nothing he could do about it, apart from being deliberately offensive occasionally.

"What did they tell really you, Jerric? When you visited them in their room?"

Jerric smiled, exposing a few teeth. He had played this game more than once before, and knew exactly what Erich felt about him. It amused him, it was always entertaining. *Poor Erich... he'd always been a fool and a fool he will die*, so he decided long ago.

"Nothing... just two Americans who came to travel in Poland. You know how it is, the Jew is trying to prove something to the Church. What's changed? What could change?"

"I don't know!" Erich steamed. "And I don't want to know! They pushed their noses into -"

"Erich, what's really bothering you?" Jerric interrupted sharply.

Erich looked at his shoes. *How does he know? How does he know all the time?* He looked at Jerric, at those predatory eyes and that shark's smile which expanded as soon as the smell of blood appeared.

"Erich? Come on, what's the story?"

Erich took a deep breath. It had to come out sometime and now was a good time as any.

"They visited the town hall."

Jerric broke into a coughing fit, surprised and annoyed. He had not expected that, and it changed many things for the worse. But he did not allow others to see it. *Erich the idiot... idiot Erich and his family...*

"You've heard this from your son? What did they want?"

"They took away all the old documents. The ones from the time of the war."

This had gone too far and there was no more reason for civilized masks. Jerric stood up angrily and almost turned the table over. The others looked at him in curiosity, which quickly turned to anger toward Erich when they realized, like Jerric, the full meaning of what he had said. Jerric, in turn, regained his temper but not a trace of anger was lost.

"I should have gotten your idiot son a place in the garbage department, not the archives."

Deep in his heart, Erich agreed. His son did not excel in being overly smart and had made many mistakes in his life. Without Jerric's help, he would have been a drunken bum in the old village, if anything. Yet still, he was his son. And in trouble.

"Don't be angry at Hans, please...he needed the money."

But Jerric was angry. Very angry. "He's an idiot - and you're an idiot!"

"No, no!"

"And what does his kid do at your place all day? Yeah, yeah," Jerric continued, "I've seen him with his gang!"

Erich closed his eyes. The worst case had come true for him: his grandson, his beloved grandson, had managed to catch Jerric's attention. And it was bad. Bad. Bad.

"Pavel, he is nothing...he is just a good boy, who takes care of his grandfather..."

"Takes care, huh? He's a neo-Nazi!"

The words exploded into the room, silencing everyone.

Silence.

Jerric sat down and poured himself some brandy, taking a mouthful. Erich joined him, but with a completely different purpose: to hide the small smile that spread across his face. *Neo-Nazi...yes, why not?*

"Forget him, Jerric," Franz intervened. "Now we have a bigger problem. This Jew will find out something."

"This Jew will not reveal anything. Someone will die before that happens."

*

The only one who died that night was a stray cat.

At first glance, it was obvious that it died from a blunt trauma to the head. The skull was busted open, shattered. But a closer examination would reveal stab wounds in different places in the fur, and even more careful examination would show its blood contained very high amounts of the feline equivalent of adrenaline.

There was a very good reason for that. For more than twenty minutes it managed to avoid the gang of skinhead youths who threw

115

at him whatever came to hand: stones, iron bars, cans. The cat was eventually trapped on top of a small tree, evading them as best he could, but finally succumbed to a well-aimed tin can.

It fell on its feet in the center circle of the boys. It tried to escape right and left, but to no avail. Everywhere he darted a kick awaited, or a nailed boot, or a waving crowbar. The fear shone from his bright yellow-green eyes, hysterical and hair-raising. These were the worst minutes in his life.

A fatal blow from an iron rod ended his life, and thus also the amusement of the boys. They looked at the silent body for several seconds, a little disappointed, a little puzzled. Pavel kicked the cat aside, smearing it on the wall of the house across the muddy street.

The well-aimed kick drew applause from the boys around him.

"Whoa... Maradona..."

They continued on, wandering through the wet streets, in their black coats and nailed boots. Pavel scraped the metal rod along a metal fence, setting off distant dogs barking. He looked at the empty beer can in his hand and crushed it. The night was young and his brain still had not enjoyed the amount of alcohol it demanded. Oh well. The pub up the road was open, and he looked at it -

And smiled.

"Let's go for a drive."

*

In the twins' room the work was in progress. Nicolas instructed Jeremiah and Isaiah to help him with the initial classification of documents, according to simple signs, which greatly accelerated the process. A second document crate was spilled across the bed, and the two brothers pounced it as if they found a treasure.

But the reward was small.

Despite the faster pace, Nicolas could not find even one significant fact that would contribute to the goal. Not a word about twins, not a word about Jews, nothing. Hours passed, and the night blackened. Downstairs the pub opened, but only a few men turned up.

Jeremiah finally looked up from the pile of documents under him, and stretched.

116

"I'm going downstairs to get a drink. Anyone want anything?" Isaiah considered joining him, but eventually gave up. Nicolas asked for a beer.

Jeremiah went downstairs, lost in thought. The cooler air in the corridor was refreshing, and he suddenly felt more liberated. Kristzah was not in her room, he noticed, and her absence reminded him of her strange performance in their room a few hours ago. *Who is she*, he asked himself? *Officially crazy?* Shuga said that she was never completely sane. He believed him. *But he also believed her.*

He went down to the middle flight of stairs, avoiding coming into view of the people sitting in the bar. He did not like the stares and although the pub was almost empty, he preferred to seek Shuga's attention without being exposed.

Shuga was not at the bar, but rather in the kitchen, further in. Jeremiah heard him rinsing glasses, and saw his white apron through the slot in the door.

He waited a few seconds.

And several more.

He finally gave up. Shuga was not going to come out soon, and it seemed silly to hide on the staircase (although every single cell in his body wanted to stay there). He was thirsty, he wanted water, and he meant to help himself.

He slowly went down another step, feeling the wood creaking under his feet. The pub was revealed to him with each step, first the nearby tables, then gradually more distant tables, some of them empty.

Finally he dropped down the last step, and was exposed to everyone else. To his delight, except for a stray look, nobody noticed him. He went to the kitchen door and opened it.

"Shuga?"

The bartender turned from the sink and turned to face him without a smile, foam on his hands. Jeremiah gave up on attempts to murmur in Polish, and just signed with his hands movements of drinking from a bottle, then pointed upward to their room. Shuga nodded and signaled *five minutes* with his fingers. Jeremiah also nodded, and smiled. No matter what language you speak, a drink was a drink, universally.

He turned to the staircase, and just before it disappeared from view, he took another one last look around at the slowly filling room.

117

A couple more people came into the pub and were greeted by their friends, who were sitting at a side table. Jeremiah was almost at the last step, but something bothered him suddenly - something that he saw outside, through the open door. He frowned and turned toward the door.

*

A cold breeze whipped his face as soon as the doors opened. It took his eyes a few seconds to become accustomed to the darkness of the night outside, but even without proper lighting he could see clearly what he had glimpsed from inside: inside their car sat a young man, maybe 20 years old, with a shaved head, playing with the wires underneath the steering wheel.

Jeremiah considered for a split second going back to call his brother and Nicolas, but decided not to. In the time it took him to run up and then come back, the car would be gone - he was quite sure. He approached the jeep with an angry cry rising in his chest.

It never came out.

Two steps before he reached the vehicle Jeremiah's eyes glazed over, and he collapsed onto the pavement. Pavel chuckled behind him, and looked at his steel rod in reappraisal. *Hey*, he smiled to himself, *I didn't even have to hit too hard.* He valued useful tools, and this bar definitely handled this *Zyd* - like the cat - in the most efficient way. Jeremiah was lying underneath him. But he was still alive - and this situation had to change.

Pavel raised the bar again.

*

The sharp scream managed to tear Miguel from his deep slumber. He got up quickly, his heart beating strongly. Eva was sitting in bed next to him, sweating, her face completely white. She got up quickly, dragging the blanket with her and dropped it to the floor. She ran into the small living room and sat by the phone.

118

She dialed a long number with shaking hands, but before she reached the end she had dropped the phone. When Miguel arrived, sleepy and confused, she dialed again.

"Eva, what...?"

"It's my father. Something's happened to him."

The call connected. Dial tone. Eva did a quick calculation in her head. It was supposed to be the afternoon now. So this would be her mother answering the phone...she hoped.

Miguel looked at her skeptically. She did not look good. Absolutely not. He began to regret the whole idea of flying to Europe. Maybe it did not help her to be outside America. Or maybe it was just the whole thing with her father, who had brought her, he suddenly realized, to the threshold of a breakdown.

"Your father? Oh, come on, Eva... you're imagining things again..."

But Eva had cut him off with a sharp glare. She returned her attention to the phone. This conversation, she knew, demanded a special delicacy.

"Mom? Hey... it's me. Whereabouts in Poland is Dad? May I have his number? No, nothing happened..."

*

But something had happened.

Jeremiah did not remember much of it. After the stars shattered behind his eyes, he met the wet floor with his cheek. Tasted the puddle. In some vague way, he knew that someone was beating him. He felt a boot stepping on his face, but did not feel pain. He felt the steel rod smashing his ribs, but not feel the sharp edges cut into his flesh. He felt the kicks at his arm, but did not know it was broken.

His vision blurred. The world swirled. Vaguely, he heard distant shouts and twisted "*Zyd*" taunts. He sighed inwardly. He had dreamed of this moment, many years ago. Dreamed the words, dreamed the shouting. He was going to die. The shot would come in a moment, then everything would go white.

Out of the corner of his eye, he saw his cell phone lying on the asphalt near the puddle. He reached toward it, seeing his hand coming slowly closer to the small black device - but then saw another hand, younger, picked it up.

Another boot punched his face.

*

Voices from the street below held no interest for Isaiah and Nicolas until the word "*Zyd*" attracted Nicolas to the window.

His eyes widened. He opened the window and yelled as loudly as he could, "Hey! Leave him alone! I'm coming down!"

Only then did Isaiah look up from the papers, and with a concerned frown he came to the window. One look was enough for him. He burst out of the room alongside Nicolas.

Luckily for Jeremiah, they were not the only ones. The lynch mob had attracted the attention of others inside the bar. And so it was that just as Isaiah and Nicolas rushed from their room, Shuga came out of the pub, waving a large knife in his hand.

Shuga was a good man.

He was not happy about the visitors he had in his hotel, certainly not after the disturbing call Jerric made to him. But dissatisfaction is one thing, and a bunch of hooligans slaughtering the *Zyd* outside his front door was quite another. He had dignity, Shuga. Besides, he hated the-

"Get out of here, vandals!"

Shuga was a big man and with a great kitchen knife flashing between the enormous belly and black stubble beard, he was able to scare off the gang of Pavel's punks. But they were not too upset. They had done what they came to do, and now they also had a new cellphone to play with.

Shuga tried to chase them, but gave up after a few meters, and settled for fist waving and throwing several juicy Polish curses. Finally, he turned and came back.

Jeremiah was lying on the road, not moving. A number of people had gathered around him, but no one dared to approach. Shuga heard someone whisper of the Jew's demise, and someone else welcomed the event.

120

The crowd was pushed aside, and Nicolas appeared next to Jeremiah. He leaned down next to him, dumbfounded. After a second Isaiah arrived as well, panting. He felt his brother's forehead. His hand came back red and wet.

"Jeremiah! Are you okay?"

No response. No movement.

Shuga came to them, the big kitchen knife still in his hand. Nicolas looked up at him, shocked.

"Who were they? Do you know?"

"Vandals. Children who should be working instead of walking around the streets. How is your Jewish friend?"

Jeremiah was breathing, but barely. He was still unconscious and his left forearm was bent at a very strange angle. Nicolas and Isaiah exchanged glances. They had to lift Jeremiah to the back room.

Nicolas went to call the doctor.

*

Cold is a strange thing. Like a high wall, it is a sharp challenge for a man. If you do not approach it with care, it will overcome you and stop you. But if you jump on it, and devour it with adrenaline and rage, it will see you further and make you feel better than ever.

The end of December was cold in Nabradosky. But to the group of boys who wandered the nighttime streets it was warm, very warm. Some threw open their heavy coats and Pavel gave his up altogether. He floated on waves of adrenaline, roared with a full throat, felt stronger than ever.

Finally he stopped, and looked around. He was in the old area of the town, close to where he had destroyed the *Zyd*'s vehicle. He looked at the neat little object in his hand again: a mobile phone, like he had only seen on TV before. Worthy loot, very worthy. Not a jeep - but still.

His gang began to gather around him with shimmering eyes and fast breathing.

"We kill him, Pavel?"

"Maybe... yeah, sure, but he's a *Zyd* - they have souls like cats."

121

But he was pretty sure the *Zyd* was dead. He heard bones crunch under his boot and saw how his eyes rolled back. The Jew was dead, he said to himself. He must be dead. And a sense of power filled him with adrenaline again, with pride. The Jew was dead! It was a reason to celebrate. He had never killed a man, true, but Jews were not really human. Right?

"We killed him, we killed him!" someone yelled next to him, followed by another one and another.

The shouts warmed Pavel's heart. He felt like he belonged. Moreover, he felt like a leader. All things considered, it was the happiest moment of his life, one he would always look back on with pride and a little envy - the first time he had allowed himself to do what he had dreamed of doing for years.

He raised his fist up.

And left it there.

Around him, slowly, the shouting died down. Mouths closed and eyes opened to look up at the raised fist. They knew what was going to happen. Knew – and couldn't believe that he would dare. Pavel's eyes flashed, drawing a wide, toothy smile all over his face, his nostrils flared. Yes, he's going to do it. He wants to do it!

He opened his palm.

A ring glittered on his finger.

"*Sieg,*" he said quietly.

"*Heil,*" came from the boys.

"*Sieg,*" he said louder.

"*Heil,*" came the answer, more confident.

"*Sieg!*"

"*Heil!*"

"*Sieg!!!*"

"*Heil!!!!!*"

The mobile phone rang.

*

And Eva went pale.

"Hello, Daddy?"

122

Miguel stood behind her, more and more worried. He did not know what to do. Fainting at the shooting range, wild dreams, and now this crazy night. Should Eva see a psychologist? He started to become more and more convinced that she should.

"Dad? Dad!"

She did not talk on the phone, but screamed at it. Desperately, crazily sobbing into the phone, she burst into tears.

That was enough for Miguel. He approached her from behind, put one hand around her chest, hugging her stomach, and with his other hand pulled the phone from her hands. This needed to be stopped, and he would put an end to it now.

"Excuse me, Mr. Neu -" he started to say into the phone.

But stopped.

At the other end was a chorus of men shouting, "*Sieg Heil*" and laughing wildly.

"Hello, who is this?" he asked, but got no response. After a second, the call was cut off.

Miguel looked at the silent device in his hand, and slowly put it on the phone rest. Eva was sitting on a chair, trembling. He hugged her, of course. But he needed a hug himself.

*

Another phone rang, waking Jerric from his slumber. Annoyed, he answered it. It was very early, too early for good news. So he listened patiently to the tense voice at the other end, and hung up after the quick goodbye.

He had new issues to deal with, it seemed.

He went to his closet and reached for the top drawer.

Yes, the gun was still there.

*

Half an hour later, the gun was cocked and aimed at Hans's temple, at the town hall. Blue fire burned in Jerric's eyes, and Hans was sweating all over, his eyes narrowed and his mouth muttered slurred apologies.

123

Finally, he did the only thing that could save his life, and in retrospect, did save him. He wet his pants.

*

Jerric could still smell fear and filth as he climbed up the stairs toward Jeremiah and Isaiah's room. The little fool would take no responsibility for his actions, just like his father - and so Jerric despised him now, just as he had learned to despise his father over the years. Some people just were made of very wimpy material.

The twins, as he already knew, were a lot tougher.

Unfortunately.

*

Unlike the first time he visited their room, this time he did not even bother to knock on the door. He just walked in like he owned the place (which was not too far from the truth).

The three musketeers, as reported by the doctor, were still in the room. Jeremiah was lying on the bed, well bandaged up and connected to an IV. Isaiah was next to him, reading from the missal. And Nicolas, unbelievably, was lying on the other bed, concentrating on the document before him.

They raised their eyes to him.

"I heard about the incident you had last night." He fixed his gaze on Jeremiah. "Is he...?"

"I will live, Jerric," Jeremiah replied weakly.

Jerric already knew this, of course. But he knew it was close. Another minute or two of such blows, he was told, and Jeremiah would be dead. He licked his lips.

"Not good, not good... you need to leave." Then he pointed to the documents, and commanded, "And these documents should be returned. Immediately."

The words cut into the room like a sharp blade, cold. This decisive tone, commanding, used by Jerric, was new to them. Until that moment he had been an old eccentric, quite harmless. But from that

124

moment he became something else entirely. Something they had not expected.

They exchanged glances. Perhaps there was something they had all missed? Apparently. Isaiah raised an eyebrow. Jeremiah shook his head.

Isaiah went to the dresser and pulled out a wallet from one of the drawers. He looked at Jerric out the corner of his eye and began to count bills: ten dollars, twenty, forty…

A cold hand reached over and closed his wallet.

"Don't even try," Jerric was almost angry. "And don't ask questions. Now start placing the documents back into boxes. Your stay in Nabradosky is over, right now."

This was completely unexpected

"What? But we got them from a town official! He -"

"That official," Jerric cut him off, "no longer works there. Now start packing, you're leaving."

Isaiah stood helpless in front of this strange, upright man, who wielded such authority. Nicolas was trying not to be seen, nor heard. But Jeremiah rose painfully to a sitting position and intervened.

"Wait a minute. Who are you? Who are you *really*?"

Jerric took a deep breath. He had not wanted to get to this point, not wanting to give them any more information, not even a negligible amount. But these were Americans. A gun to the head wouldn't necessarily work on them. But common sense, combined with legal authority could make a difference here. Americans were a law-abiding people. Normally.

"My name," he hesitated a split second before he continued, examining them with his eyes, "is Jerric Kosoto, former mayor of Nabradosky. To be precise, I was mayor of Nabradosky throughout the Soviet period."

Jerric was right.

The twins certainly looked at him in a new way, more appreciatively. They were more open to him, maybe even open to instructions. That's what he liked about Americans. Although it seemed as if they like their freedom (and the rest of the democratic yadda yadda) what talked to Americans most was authority.

125

"These documents... you got them illegally. Not that I care about that - not at all! But they are government property, and tourists have no business with them."

Isaiah considered this solemnly. He knew, of course, the man was right. They did, after all, 'buy' these documents in a very illegal (but very acceptable here, most likely) way. Indeed, in a true state of law, they had no right to hold them. Certainly not after someone officially demanded their return. But...

"You're here on official business?"

Jerric had anticipated these words beforehand.

"No. But if I know that you have the files, other people - more official - will know about it as well. It's not healthy for you all. Especially for you," he indicated Jeremiah.

The implicit threat had not slipped Isaiah's attention. The man, it turned out, was deadly serious. Too serious for a few bits of worthless paper.

"What's so special about these documents?"

"Nothing. Mainly municipal bills, taxes, population registry... nothing special."

"So why keep them a secret?"

Jerric took a deep breath. He was not used to being challenged - and his morning had begun much earlier than he liked. Did these people really not understand what was going on around them?

"You ever visited a Soviet state?"

"No," admitted Isaiah. "But you are no longer a Soviet state."

"Officially, no."

The words hung in the air a bit. Isaiah considered how to continue the conversation. Jeremiah remained silent. For now.

"And practically?"

"Practically, there are procedures. Some people will keep those procedures."

It is not pleasant to be threatened, to be intimidated, Jeremiah thought. Then he remembered the pain in his hand and ribs, and decided that there are even less pleasant things. He exchanged a heavy look with Isaiah. He felt the sheer negativity in the outlined shake of his chin. Jerric also sensed it, apparently, and changed tactics.

"You have to understand. I'm here to protect you. Help you."

126

Jeremiah could not bear it any more.

"Then help us!" he snapped. "Don't lie to us! What, if there even was a name, was this village called at that time? You were mayor, you should know!"

He could have said much more, if not for the sharp pain in his ribs, which stopped him. He could not take a deep breath, nor shout.

"Jerric?" he asked, faintly.

But Jerric was elsewhere. His gaze fell to the floor, then to his shoes. He noticed a spot of mud on the black, shiny leather. He would have to clean it off later, he thought. He would give the mud time to harden. It would be easier to remove it then.

"Jerric? Have you forgotten?"

The words penetrated his consciousness, and he returned to the room. But not as he went in a few minutes ago. Jeremiah and Isaiah also could sense the change. The tension in his shoulders disappeared, his posture relaxed. He was no longer Jerric the Almighty Mayor. He went back to being the old, sick man they met in the woods, standing before a silent mound of rocks.

"Bielisk. It was called Bielisk."

He sat on a nearby chair. Suddenly he felt the morning cold even more, the weight of his old bones. A new pain attacked his back, a pain that he had not felt before that day. Old age. He hated to be reminded of its existence.

Jeremiah tried to remind him of other things.

"Bielisk? A Jewish name it, isn't it?"

Inwardly, Jerric cried. Outwardly he just smiled wearily.

"Jewish? No, no, no, no, no - not Jewish. It's a pure Polish name."

For the first time since Jerric entering the room, Nicolas made his presence known.

He turned a page over.

But just this brief sound was enough to make Jeremiah look at him. Nicolas looked back at him with a look that said one word: lie.

"No Jews ever lived here?"

Jerric was too tired to notice those signs.

"No, no. I told you."

Jeremiah smiled. There was something significant here and he intended to get to the bottom of it. He opened his mouth to continue the investigation - but Isaiah put his hand up and spoke for him in a concluding tone of voice.

"Okay, if you say so - we believe you. Nicolas, did we finish looking into these documents?"

Nicolas spread his hands helplessly.

"I'd like to devote a few more hours to it, but from what I've seen here - the first records starting the population survey were conducted in 1940. I saw the name of Mr. Kosoto here many times. In this poll too (he indicated the papers in his hand). But... there is no record of twins who were born or died in 1944."

Jerric was glad to hear this answer. It was expected, of course. And though he tried to keep a straight face, something of a sigh escaped him.

Jeremiah picked up on it, and his body went rigid with anger. He wanted so much to speak - but his brother's hand warned him against saying even one more word. With some frustration, he decided to let Isaiah run the show.

"And any Jews?" He pressed Nicolas.

"No record of any Jews."

Isaiah nodded, and turned to Jeremiah with a smile.

"Well, then, looks like we're in the wrong village. We made inquiries and received answers. So, then, we have no more reason to hold these documents, right?"

Jeremiah's eyes flashed with anger and amazement. But he was silent. Isaiah thanked him with a nod and smile, turning back to Jerric.

"If so, we'll return the documents immediately at the beginning of next week."

The satisfied expression that had been building on Jerric's face in the last few moments was wiped off in a split second. If there was anything Jerric did not like (apart from idiots) it was being lied to to his face. And in a single moment he was the aggressive mayor again.

"Today. It must be today." His threatening tone caused Isaiah to take a half-step back, but not enough to wipe the peaceful smile off his face. Secretly, Isaiah thanked God that he had given enough masses and sermons in front of a hostile crowd that he could keep up his facade.

"Okay... so today. Of course."

Jerric watched him carefully for a few long seconds, until he was convinced the priest in front of him was actually telling the truth. *That was too easy, wasn't it?* But he was tired, very tired. The person who had entered the room twenty minutes ago would never have bought it. But people are less inclined to argue when they are tired.

"Well," he sighed at last. "I'll tell the clerks to expect you before the end of the day."

"Thank you," replied Isaiah. "That's so good of you." It was a mistake.

Tired or not, Jerric could not ignore this thick sarcastic tone. For a split second he was that powerful person again. Then he softened up.

"It may be difficult for you to believe it, my son, but I really am doing it for you." There was sadness in his voice. He continued, "Bring the documents to the town hall, then just leave the place. Quickly."

And just as he arrived, Jerric left.

*

They listened to Jerric's heavy footsteps as they moved away, slowly disappearing down the stairs. A number of seconds passed in total silence, and then —

"What's the matter with you? We haven't finished checking the papers..."

Isaiah expected this angry outburst from his brother, and answered him in the same quiet passion.

"What planet are you on, Jeremiah? We're not safe here. Let's go while we still can."

Nicolas chose to intervene. He whispered calmly, "You know, the documents here really make no mention of Jews..."

"Of course they don't!" Isaiah cried out loudly. "Because they're fake. Imitation. A scam!"

Jeremiah and Nicolas looked at him, petrified.

129

"All this," he continued, gesturing at the scattered papers, "is a big fat fake! We won't find anything here, even if we look for years."

He concluded his remarks, and looked at his search partners.

"But," Nicolas finally responded, "these papers are old. Whether it's a fake..."

"So it must be an old fake. An antique fake. And this Jerric... he scares me."

Not just him. Nicolas himself was still stunned at Jerric's aggressive invasion of their privacy and room; he gave orders, he radiated power. Jerric was, he felt in his Polish bones, one of the old dinosaurs of the old Soviet era. One of those who made people disappear, people they did not like. There was something military in him. Something disturbing.

Jeremiah, in turn, was concerned about other things. He looked at the pile of documents. Despite making a lot of progress that day, they still had two more unopened boxes. *What was in them that made the old man so jumpy?*

"Jerric is scared. Of us."

Now it was Isaiah's turn to frown.

"What do you mean?"

"Look: why's he insisting we give the documents back - and tonight? What is he trying to hide?"

Isaiah and Nicholas had no answer. Jeremiah looked at them and decided for them.

"We're going to continue examining the documents. *All* the documents."

Revelations

"As when one cleaveth and breaketh up the earth, our bones are scattered at the grave's mouth." (Psalms 141:7)

They dived into more documents, Nicolas leading, the brothers close behind. Document after document, years after year. Numbers meant flesh and clothing, words became born living creatures that lived, married, died and were buried.

World War II was at the bottom of the fourth box, and brought with it a new type of document, darker, less orderly. Cannons were fired. Borders were breached, mixed with blood and pain. People were shot and killed. Money was issued, hoarded, stolen and burned. Buildings were destroyed. Babies born. Tombs excavated.

But none of them had twins.

*

She did not report to anyone. She left no message, not to her direct commander, nor to her family. Only Miguel was in on the secret, sworn to try his best to cover up her departure. He did indeed help her get away, though he was so concerned for her that half an hour after Eva had left the base, he had the phone in his shaking hand, dialling headquarters, only to hang up.

And she knew it.

She had not expected to pass with a nod through the guard post at the exit from the base.

She did not expect to get a taxi so easily, did not she expect her cell phone to stay quiet for four hours.

In fact, only after the plane had taken off for Warsaw without suffering any delays, was she sure Miguel had really kept his word. *He really loved her.*

The flight attendant issued all the necessary safety instructions, and Eva Neumann fell asleep.

*

Dreams came almost immediately. The images were more colorful than ever. She found herself fleeing the black forests and frozen meadows, with cannon roars in the background and the noise of crashing metal trampling all other sounds.

She saw how people crumpled, shot in the back of the neck. Heard screaming women and wailing bullets. She scurried from tree to tree, staring into cold human eyes, her emotions running free. Hot tears melted into the ice, and severe pain shook her whole body. She was in several places simultaneously, saw many horrors at the same time.

The dreams had a life, they were close. Wild laughter was contorted with rage and bitter tears. Aircraft buzzed overhead, sending death packets to the scorched earth. Grease mingled with the smell of gunpowder, and rivers of blood erupted from holes in human corpses. An explosion assaulted her ears.

Babyish cries came from between her hands, and the noise grew louder, striking her ears sharply, becoming painful, penetrating and pressing on her eardrums.

*

"What?"

Eva awoke slowly, a metallic taste in her mouth and panic in her stomach. Pressure! A sharp pain snapped at her ears, so she quickly sealed her nostrils with her fingers and exhaled sharply with her mouth closed.

Relief.

The intense pain gave way to the increasing noise of the aircraft engines. Distant lights were visible under the dark shape of the wings and there was the usual stirring among the passengers. Landing in Warsaw was imminent and a nasal male voice announced in two languages that the temperature outside was about minus 5 Celsius.

Eva wiped the sweat from her forehead.

*

"Hey... I need to - "

"No, no English... Polish? Russian? Deutsch?"

"*Deutsch ist gut. Ich möchte nace Nabradosky gehen.*"

Much sucking through teeth and shaking of the head: "*Nabradosky...es ist einem lange weg...*"

133

Eva took out a green bill, and the taxi driver nodded and started the engine. Slightly above the horizon winked a small flash of lightning, too far away for sound.

*

Their windows rattled violently, and Nicolas thought for a moment they would shatter. But they held out, and he returned to another old meaningless document. Was it the thousandth document he had read that day, or maybe the ten thousandth? He did not know. He sank into the mechanical routine of scanning for keywords within yellowing documents, as he had learned in high school in Gdansk, and at the University of Warsaw.

Nicolas was used to reading. He studied law at university, having to fight for every Zloty in order to survive on the demanding campus. His family, he knew, could not help him. On the contrary, they were dependent on him making a success of himself. So he passed his days in the focused, well-maintained library of the university, and his nights as a junior waiter and dishwasher at a nice restaurant in the Stare Miasto.

It was not much - but it was enough for him to finish the fourth year of the degree, and soon he hoped to get an internship in a good law firm. Thinking ahead, he chose to specialize in English knowing it was a strong suit for him. Poland was still scorched land for foreign investors. But they would come, it was crystal clear. If they could open a McDonald's near Red Square, they would also come to Poland.

And Nicolas would be there at the right time to connect them up with the Polish bureaucracy. He would be there in just the right place to maneuver them through the tangle of rigid rules and channel the lubrication funds to the most important screw in the bureaucratic machine.

And his first customers, he was happy to say, were here in his hands. Two twins with their strange story, with religious fervor in their eyes, with their fears... he was there by chance on the first day they landed in Warsaw, and overheard them discussing their search.

How surprised they were to hear their waiter turn to them in fluent English, and offer his aid. How happy they were to hear about his law

134

degree, and how happy they were to pull out their wallets and buy at least six months of freedom from washing dishes. (Halleluiah!) This was the cost of a guided tour deep into the country, all expenses paid by them.

He agreed, of course. But not before hustling for a fancy price of which they were happy to pay half in advance.

He expected, of course, all kinds of such problems, especially with the Jew, who seemed to have quite suspicious eyes and seemed... not clean, if he wanted to be completely honest with himself. But he did not expect him to almost get killed. He did not expect the presence of a frightening secret policeman there. (Though he was listed as mayor, Nicolas was willing to bet his life that Jerric did something much deeper and military-related than just that.)

He also did not expect their car to be virtually written off, and that no one would be willing to fix it. He had purchased plastic bags and sealed the broken windows, but the jeep became almost impossible to drive in the rain and was certainly very unpleasant.

He now found himself lying on the bed on this dark afternoon, going over documents, and blinking whenever lightning pierced the sky outside the window. He did not like it. He was afraid, even. The noise was like a giant whip, and whenever it happened the air in the room filled with a pungent scent and the little hairs on the back of his neck stood up. Despite the heat, he shivered.

He had another two documents to read from the box, the last but one.

"That's it. We're done," Isaiah announced.

Nicholas looked up, surprised. Jeremiah also was surprised and a little angry.

"Excuse me?"

"Town hall's about to close," Isaiah said. "We need to return the documents."

"But... we haven't finished checking everything."

"And probably never will."

"You can't..." continued Jeremiah.

"I can and I will!"

The thunder that came from Isaiah's throat echoed around the walls of the room. His eyes watered.

135

"Don't you understand?" His voice was suddenly pleading. "It's too dangerous. There is a limit. I waited fifty-two years to get to know you - and now to lose you..." He turned to Nicolas. "Start packing. We're leaving."

But Jeremiah did not agree.

"No. I will not," he said quietly, trustingly. "I want to know who burned down my house. I want to know who killed my parents. I want to know who. And I want to know why."

His determination, his calm face, the steel in his voice, caused Isaiah to look at him helplessly. His twin brother lay there on the bed, with a broken body, but with an uncompromising desire to achieve what he came there to accomplish. *While he, Isaiah could go about freely - but would rather flee for his life. Where did this difference come from - where?*

"Maybe it's better to go, Jeremiah."

"No. I will not run away. Not without knowing the truth."

"It's not worth it! Robert White was right. It's just not worth it."

They stared at each other, glaring.

"God... look at this," Nicolas whispered suddenly into the silence. The rain's noise stopped. For a moment, no lightning pierced the sky lighting the small room. A wintry silence fell on Nabradosky. Even the wind that wailed through the tall forest trees, went silent and suddenly became expectant. There was electricity in the air.

Every hair on the back of his neck stood on end as Jeremiah took the yellow document from Nicolas. It was a relatively big map of Nabradosky, folded into four equal parts. It was a very old map. 1946, it said in its title. In 1946...

Jeremiah looked at it. He did not see anything special. Nicolas pointed his finger to a remote point at the edge of the map. His finger slid slowly over the thick edge folds and picked out a sketch of the town's cemetery. A large cross was drawn in two thick black lines. Jeremiah looked at the cross, still not understanding. But then when Nicolas drew back his finger, as if apologizing, he revealed two tiny words, handwritten in blue ink. Two words straining to hide - and still trying to attract attention.

Jeremiah did not understand the handwritten words, but the small icon next to them, he understood more. By the light of a particularly protracted flash of lightning that illuminated the room with a bright white light, Jeremiah made out a small Star of David sign.

And began to cry.

The thunder came a split second after the first hot drop accumulated at the edge of his eyes. Isaiah tried to say something, but even he could not hear himself. The room shifted from the intensity of the noise and a huge barrage of rain threatened to break into the room. Isaiah decided not to repeat himself, glad his words were swallowed up.

"What..." Jeremiah then asked quietly, "What is written here?"

Nicholas did not hear it, only saw his lips moving slightly. Still, he knew what the question was, knew what the important thing was.

"Help. Here."

Jeremiah put the map away from him, and Isaiah picked it up. The rain's noise quietened a little allowing them to talk, albeit loudly.

"It's so small," said Nicholas. "I almost missed it."

Isaiah looked at again and again at the little blue marks.

There are truths that we do not want to find out, he thought to himself again and again, with a strong sense of *déja vu. There are truths that are better not to be found. There are wounds in which it is better not to pry.*

"That's what we were looking for," Jeremiah said triumphantly. "This is proof."

*

This last thunder clap was the loudest of them all, so much so that it managed to wake Jerric from the disturbed afternoon nap into which he had unwittingly sunk very deeply. He was alone in the house, he knew. The woman had gone to her friends, or so she told him. He no longer cared. Maybe some fifty years ago, he thought.

Thunder shook the walls of the house, and woke him.

There was something he had to do, he now knew.

*

His bones ached. They always did in the winter in this bloody country. He wanted to go home. At his bedside was a bottle of

137

cognac. He drank a sip. Then he rose and went to make tea. Anything to get rid of the pain in his cursed bones. The house was warm, true. But it did not help the pain.

He boiled a pot of water for the tea, holding his old hands near the burning flames. As always, he felt nothing. His skin was too thick, or the edges of his nerves were already burned out. Like his body. Like his memory. Wait a minute... *there was something he had to do.*

He cursed softly: the documents.

The phone was in the other room, and Jerric rushed toward it. The first number he dialed was a mistake, and he cursed and called it again.

A sleepy male voice answered. Jerric barked a question at him and received a reply. He slammed the phone down.

Lightning lit up the house. The kettle began to whistle, but Jerric did not hear it. Instead, he went back and forth, back and forth, wandering between the walls. He considered all the other options. He went over them again and again, trying to look for any crack in them, some defect. He found many. But it did not matter to him. Either way, this story would end tonight.

He felt some relief. He went back to the phone and began to dial.

*

As she had done during the flight, on the long drive to Nabradosky Eva fell into a stormy sleep. The driver, out of consideration for his passenger, lowered the radio's volume - and then, after experiencing her snoring, turned it back up. She was beautiful. Very beautiful; he looked at the American girl hungrily.

She was deep in her dream. Her eyes darted from side to side, occasionally a slight sigh escaped her mouth. She was beautiful. Very pretty. As the sky darkened and the roads emptied, he fought the urge to caress her cheek - or maybe more.

But something about her made him cringe .In the light of distant lightning, the taxi kept going.

*

They arrived at the cemetery with their headlights off.

Nobody understood why Isaiah turned off the lights in the middle of the road, not even Isaiah himself. But nobody challenged it. Lights turned off, the road was dark, and the old cemetery of Nabradosky swallowed them without witnesses.

Only when the open gate was behind them, and the few street lights disappeared behind the wall, did he dare to turn the lights on again.

A long row of graves appeared before him, a silent line. Headstones came out of the ground, crosses engraved on them. Some gravestones were in the form of a cross. Some were white, others black. Some had the deceased's picture etched on.

Nicolas shuddered.

Isaiah turned off the engine but left the headlights turned on. Blessed silence enveloped them, merging with the white noise of the rain, washing the car with a steady sound. The thick plastic sheeting did its work well: barely a drop penetrated the vehicle, though you could not say the same about the cold.

Lightning pierced the sky, chased by rumbles of thunder. Without a word the three men prepared to exit the vehicle. Raincoats were added over the thick coats they wore. The doors shut with a bang and the trunk was soon open, spewing out two shovels and three flashlights.

Jeremiah held his broken arm. He was in a lot of pain.

"We're far enough away from the town. Very good."

The agreement of his companions came as silence. Nicolas studied the shovel in his hand, weighing it. At the hardware store he bought it from, he could not bring himself to ask questions. The heavyset shopkeeper gave him the two shovels with a cold stare, almost frightening. He had at least checked the flashlights were working before he fled for his life.

"You know," he joked without humor, "when you hired me you didn't say anything about digging graves at night, in the rain."

"You're right. You don't have to come with us."

Jeremiah, it seemed, was much more serious than Nicolas. But you could not blame him. He could not understand how this new discovery deeply touched the heart of the young Pole. The little Star of David mark on the map shocked Nicolas more than one would imagine. For the first time since he had met the twins, he felt that they had a point.

If anything, he wanted to be the one to reveal it.

So he just smiled, gently patted the rabbi's shoulder and shone his flashlight on the old map.

"There," he pointed out and led the brothers to the fence over the other side.

*

Two hours and six holes later, Nicolas leaned on the fence and wiped the moisture from his brow. Rain or sweat? A mixture of both, probably. He was soaked inside and out, sweating inside his heavy clothing, and from the bad weather that refused to move on.

He was tired, but he knew that if he rested more than a minute or two, he would get cold. So he raised his shovel again, and began digging his seventh hole, inches to the right of the sixth hole.

By a flash of lightning he saw Isaiah doing the same, with heavier movements but also more determined. Stick it in the ground. Place your foot. Push it. Draw its heavy load. So it worked. Imbed it in the ground. Put a foot on. Stand. Draw. Press. Foot. Stand. Draw.

Jeremiah looked on with a certain envy. He wanted so much to help them with the excavation, but could not. He could barely walk, and if his doctor knew that he was on his feet out in the cold like that, he would certainly be hospitalized and in a psychiatric ward. But the bitter cold was a certain advantage: it dulled the pain to a minimum, pushing it to the edge of his consciousness.

Still, Jeremiah knew he was going to pay dearly for this night. He was no longer young, and his injuries had weakened him. The icy grip of this intense cold would not leave his bones quickly, he knew. He was going to suffer a lot because of it.

But not now, not yet.

He looked at the map again, at the tiny lettering that brought them here so late. He looked, examined and shook his head. A tiny voice of reason whispered to him that they should have already found whatever was there, if it *really* was there.

140

He brushed the little voice aside. Reason had no place there, in the cemetery, that stormy night. Only faith. He looked at the newly dug pits that were filling with water quickly.

"I don't understand, it has to be here!" he shouted against the wind.

"Maybe it's buried deeper," Nicolas shouted back at him. "I'll try to dig deeper."

"Try! We must find it tonight!"

And to demonstrate solidarity with them, he turned his flashlight along the fence, looking for something, some sign, some clue that would lead them to...

To his mother.

He suddenly knew that he was looking for her. That she was... she was the one who wrote the words on the map. His heart pounded hard, and new sweat sprouted on his back. The rain whispered groggy secrets and the flashlight skipped across the old crosses and worn marble slabs. His feet took him along the fence, navigating between dug trenches and stumps of dead trees.

The flashlight suddenly paled against the electric flash that ripped the sky open. For a long second the world was lit brighter than day, and before his eyes burned a pile of white stones piled up at the corner of the fence.

The lightning ceased, and the world darkened and thundered.

*

When the sounds returned to his ears, he was standing by the next pile of worn marble. In the round circle of the flashlight, the old stones were just old stones, lacking any distinction or shine. He examined them more closely, from different angles.

Nothing.

Just stones. Old marble, unused. He had already turned to go, when his eye was caught by a broken marble slab that revealed an unusual configuration of etched lines.

One line... that connected to another line, at an angle of sixty degrees, in a way that a cross was never configured. Before his wet

141

eyes formed a familiar form, a triangle. A familiar form, and under it the familiar words in a familiar language...

"... Elijah Leib Ybe pinha..."

Jeremiah's cry thundered over the storm.

*

Eva awoke from her restless sleep again, slick with sweat.

The taxi driver looked at her anxiously. This was already the second time on this trip that she had done so. Her eyes were wide, dark pits staring ahead.

"Everything all right?" he asked.

"Yes. Keep going."

And he kept going. Suddenly he realized that he actually had spoken to her in Polish, not German. It was weird. Not only did she understand the language, but she answered him in fluent Polish. He turned to smile at her to ask her about it.

But her eyes were elsewhere.

*

They were in the cemetery on a night of roaring thunder and lightning. And she was wet. Soulfully wet, cold to the deepest of her bones. She was wearing only a light coat, completely unseasonable, and light shoes that easily drowned in the mud.

She looked around nervously. Had she recognized movement? No, it was just the reflection of the lightning over the marble monument. She hated these tombstones, the new ones - cross-shaped headstones, crossed tombstones, Christian symbols that ruled over graves that were not theirs. For a moment she wanted to break them apart, but then again she recalled her intended purpose, and closed her hands around a small tin box.

This was once her jewelry box, once, when she had a life. Today, all that remained of her life lay in this little treasure box, this Moses box that she was to launch on the river of history.

The rain stung her flesh, but that did not matter to her. Soon, she knew, she would die anyway, and her wet predicament was an advantage. It made the hard ground turn into black mud, which would be easy to dig with only bare hands. But

142

where to dig the hole? She looked left and right, and then her eyes fixed on one point, by a hidden corner of the fence, which was piled up with old marble remains. She began to dig.

*

Isaiah was forced to pull Jeremiah to his feet almost by force, finding him mired in the mud trying to dig with his hands. Strange, but Isaiah had a tremendous urge to actually join him. Something in the ground called him, pulled him. He wanted to dig!

But instead he raised his wounded twin brother.

"What are you doing?"

"There is a Jewish gravestone here! This *was* a Jewish cemetery."

Isaiah looked around. All the tombs were constructed in the form of a cross. And yet...

"Jewish?"

"Yes, you see..."

And he pointed to the broken marble fragment carved with the Star of David. Isaiah shone his flashlight on the spot, but the rain blurred the exact contours of the inscription on the monument.

He approached the marble, and stuck his shovel in the ground in order to use both hands. But it was not enough.

But instead of the moist squelch of a steel blade penetrating the heavy soil, a soft metallic muffled click sounded. The shovel, unable to penetrate the ground, fell into a shallow puddle created beside it.

Nicolas reached into the ground, and picked out a small iron box, covered with mud. Jeremiah shone his flashlight on it, but need not have bothered. A huge flash of sheet lightning floodlit the ground while a sudden burst of rain washed the box, leaving it clean.

*

Nicolas rushed to shield the box using his umbrella. Jeremiah held his flashlight up and Isaiah tried to open its clasp - an act that turned out to be relatively easy.

The case was very old and very rusty. It was coated with a black substance that disintegrated in his hands - grease, guessed Isaiah, and

143

he was correct. There was brown wax paper inside. It was obvious that whoever had set it in the ground knew it would have to go through at least one winter.

Or fifty, he thought.

And it seemed that this was the last winter the box would have been able to go through unscathed. Time was about to overcome the iron and wax paper. The interior was very moist but not flooded.

With numb and petrified fingers, Isaiah carefully withdrew the objects buried in the box: multiple metal ornaments, a gold medal and a piece of folded paper.

Isaiah's movements froze for a moment. All three could easily identify the metal objects...still, as they looked at the evil shiny objects and old, ancient horror crept into them, sinking deeper.

Finally, Isaiah put the metal objects in the box, and gently opened the folds of the letter. After a brief moment, he handed it to Nicolas.

"I don't know," he replied after a timeless minute or so. "Everything's blurred and in small writing here... I can identify just a few words: *fast... killed* - or *kill*, I don't know... there's a few names: *Abram Goldblum... Ijo Krinitzy*... that's all. Signed down here *Helena Goldblum*."

The last name hit Jeremiah like a hammer. He knew. He just knew.

Isaiah was also experiencing the same electric current. He had never heard that name before - and yet, he knew it was his. He had never ever thought of it - and yet, it struck a chord in him.

Helena Goldblum.

That was her name.

With a shake of his head, he turned his attention back to the box, back to those bright metallic items, the likes of which he had only seen in history books.

He took the first one, the larger, in his hand.

By the light of flashes sheeting across the sky, he turned the swastika in his hand, bright and shining, again and again.

*

A second. Two seconds. Three seconds.

The lightning stopped, but the light remained.

Even the thunder which had crashed above the cemetery for a good minute was gone, though the noise continued to roll over the cemetery.

Jeremiah lifted his head.

He was looking straight at three vehicles with their high beams illuminating the place, dazzling them all. Dark shadows came out of the vehicles and approached them, holding rifles, the engine sounds integrating into the loud metallic clattering of the rifles.

He looked at the scene paralyzed, unable to speak or move. Suddenly, everything seemed completely surreal - not just the past few minutes, but all that had happened to him since he had got the letter from the hospital, the letter informing him of the existence of his twin brother. Everything seemed so unreal, detached like the remote hallucinogenic twilight of dreams that are experienced just before the morning.

The bright lights, the engine sounds, the smell of the heavy soil, the thunderclaps over the tombstones... what was he doing here, Jeremiah asked himself. What was he doing here, in this godforsaken place, instead of being with his family, with everything he loved?

The cold clung to his bones.

The shadows approached him, and one black arm reached out and took the metal box from him.

"Thank you," said a familiar voice. "We've been looking for this for quite some time, you know."

Another lightning flash lit up the cemetery, dimming the car's headlights. For one long moment, all the people around there were illuminated with the same intensity, to the same level of accuracy and clarity.

Jeremiah was not surprised.

"Jerric."

But it was not just Jerric. Four men surrounded them besides him, all in their seventies or older, and armed with weapons at least as ancient as they were. Jeremiah was able to identify several faces: these were the same people sitting at Jerric's side in the pub when they arrived in Nabradosky.

Isaiah also recognized them, but his attention was fully on Jerric. He was the leader of the group, he was sure. In the lightning flash, his

145

teeth shimmered with his shark-like smile, determined-looking. His movements were flexible and young, almost catlike, and Isaiah could not help but be filled with genuine fear of this young old man, who aimed a black, well-oiled rifle carelessly at them.

Nicolas, for his part, almost burst out laughing at the group of elderly Poles pointing World War II rifle relics. On the other hand, it seemed like they knew what to do with their weapons. They were connected, he knew, to the Nazi objects that they had found, one way or another.

Jerric backed up a bit, watching the light metal decorations under the flashlight. His face took on an almost greedy look as his fingers groped the swastika, and even more so when he examined the other medallion, which was in the form of a steel eagle.

If Jerric's feelings were masked by a shark-like smile, Erich was the antithesis: he almost went mad at the sight of the Nazi symbols.

"Look, look," he spewed out in excited German. "Like old times!"

He stretched, gave a Nazi salute, and in front of Jeremiah's astonished eyes pinned the symbol on his coat.

Jerric grinned at Erich's excitement, but it was not the place and certainly not the time.

"Take it off, you idiot!" he shot harshly, "and stop speaking German!"

"But Jerric, who will know? There's no one here!"

Jerric was about to answer him harshly, but Franz, holding a Mauser, stepped between them with a smile.

"Let him have some fun... so many years have passed since..."

Jerric thought for a second, then dismissed the matter. Before him were bigger problems and more difficult decisions - decisions that he knew were hard, very hard, to make. And he was angry. So angry. Angry about the rain. Angry about the cold. Angry about the group of parasites that surrounded him. And most of all - angry at the three lunatics standing before him, still holding their shovels.

"Idiots!" he snapped at them in English, and slammed his fist into Isaiah's face. "Tell me, what are you doing here? After I warned you!"

Isaiah staggered, but did not fall. Something warm was dripping from his nose.

"We had to find out what happened to our parents."

146

"You had to, eh? You'll discover all right. Definitely, you're going to find out."

Erich frowned and stepped forward. He did not like to hear conversations in a language he did not know, even if they were accompanied by some satisfying punches in the right direction. He was cold and wet and his finger on the trigger began to freeze.

"What do we do with them, Jerric?"

Jerric ran different scenarios through his mind again, calculated actions and reactions. Again, he tested scenarios, tried to make the circles into squares again. Like all his deliberations during the last hours, the results were the same. It would be a problem to cover it up. It would be a problem to explain it. He might even pay for it with his life. But he would have to do the inevitable.

He shone his flashlight on the shovels, and then the pits already excavated.

"This is a cemetery isn't it?"

*

Boom!

The sound of a single shot flicked Eva's ear, waking her up into an unstable reality.

Boom Boom Boomboomboomboomboomboomboom-

The sound came back in a strong rumble that rolled somewhere under her seat, accompanied by screeching wheels. The taxi zigzagged wildly between lanes, almost flipping over.

Eva gripped the seat with both hands, glad of the seat belt she had pulled on out of habit at the beginning of the trip. The driver, who had looked at her with disdain and disbelief, fought the steering wheel hard right now, all the while giving out juicy Polish curses.

Now the taxi was completely in the wrong lane, spinning in place, now the left wheels were up in the air, then landing with a thud, crashing onto the road.

Silence.

"What happened?"

"The tire blew."

147

The driver got out of the taxi and into the storm, and Eva released the seat belt and went after him.

She looked around. The night was very wet, but not really dark. The thunderstorm wounded the dark sky with electrical streaks every few seconds and lit the thick forest which extended on both sides of the road. Far up the road she saw the lights of a town.

She turned to the driver, who was busy assessing the damage to the car, raising her voice above the storm.

"Tell me, where are we?"

"Outside Nabradosky. A few more minutes and we would be there."

The tire was completely destroyed. The driver did not think there would be a problem resuming the journey, although he hated changing tires. Certainly in the rain, that made it all slippery and dangerous to his numbed fingers. Either way, there was little choice. He opened the trunk and took out the jack and the spare tire.

He was very careful when he lifted the car on the jack, and rightly so. His first attempt almost ended in a broken hand when the rain caused the metal rod to slide and fall down. He cursed softly, wiped a little rain off his forehead, and tried again. This time things were a little more stable, and the battle arena moved to the locking bolts of the wheel which refused to move under the wrench.

After twenty minutes of concentrated effort, he strengthened his foothold on the fourth bolt and threw the broken wheel to the side of the road. Rain or not, Nabradosky was close, and payment for this damn journey would buy him at least one night of freedom, if not more. The American tourist had paid nearly double the true fare. This was good! Sadly, replacing the wheel was just as hard.

He rose to his feet, smiling.

"Well, we can continue to - "

But Eva was no longer around.

*

The trees. The trees!

They were so familiar, so foreign. Her eyes were half closed, and yet she went on, running between the wet leaves and tree trunks. Her

148

foot slipped twice on the water-soaked earth, but she got up quickly and continued to run forward.

She did not know where she was going, she did not know why. The weeping of a baby echoed in her ears, urging her forward. A strong sense of urgency formed in her chest, and tears sprang from her eyes. *Come on! Come on!*

She no longer knew who she was.

Nor was she afraid to know.

*

"So, that's how you intend to kill us? Like you murdered our parents?"

Jeremiah groaned with pent up pain. He could stand, so he was forced to dig, slowly, in a lot of pain, but rigidly determined. He rejected Isaiah's offer of help. *No one will dig my grave. Certainly not my brother.*

Isaiah, for himself, was empty of thoughts. He recalled the moment when he first saw his twin brother, a long-bearded rabbi in the middle of his church. When was that? Eons ago? Another life, in another world.

Nicolas was too angry to think. Fifty years after the fact, and still he was standing, a Pole in Poland, digging a grave for himself at Nazi gunpoint. Fifty years later!

"You brought this on yourself," Jerric spewed out at last. "I warned you —"

"You're murderers! And you're fools! You think you can do this without being noticed?"

We've been doing it for fifty years, Jerric thought to himself. But times have changed. You can't eliminate people now without someone paying for it... or maybe you can? He toyed with various ideas. But no, he decided again. *They know too much. Too much.*

Jeremiah weakly threw his shovel into the pit.

"Come on. Do it."

But Jerric was in no hurry. He shone his flashlight into the gaping wound in the earth. *Not big enough,* he decided. A glimpse into the pits dug by Isaiah and Nicolas told him they were both ready...but it was not enough.

"Keep digging there," he ordered Nicolas, and the young Pole reluctantly moved forward.

"*Schnell!*" he snapped, surprising himself in German.

Nicolas stuck the shovel in the ground and continued from where Jeremiah stopped.

"Who are you?" Isaiah asked simply.

Jerric did not answer. He just watched the tomb growing deep in the damp soil, noticing how the lightning whitened the wet clothes and how the rain disappeared into the black hole.

"It was German, right?" insisted the priest.

Jerric lazily turned his attention to Isaiah, who stood and stared at him. There was pain in that gaze. Pain...and understanding. For a moment, Isaiah's merciful, loving gaze pulled Jerric back to other brighter days...distant days. *He understood him, damn it*. And that understanding frightened Jerric. He could not return the priest's gaze.

"You can still confess, my son."

Jerric chuckled sadly, and returned to the cold reality, the dark reality. *Confession... I missed my chance*. Anyway, the whole situation suddenly seemed very funny. Starting with the old rifles dating from a life that had long since gone, pulled out from an ancient hiding place (*who would have thought, eh?*) to this serious priest, who was digging a grave for himself now - and was still trying to save his soul.

"They're done," Erich cut in. "Should we do it?"

"In a minute."

He had things to do. Things to say. Things to hear. Was there time left? He looked at the three graves. Dug well, deep enough. Perfect for hiding the truth, burying it, this time for good.

Yes, the time had passed.

"So. Stand there, please, by the... holes."

Jerric cocked his rifle again.

"I'm sorry."

Jeremiah swallowed. His heart started racing. White light filled his pupils, and the words began to escape from his lips: "Lord our God, the Lord is one..."

A single shot pierced the air.

Then another. And another one.

Cries of pain... machine gun fire... and the pungent scent of gunpowder.

*

The shots were very close to her, and one of the bullets scorched a line that passed right next to her right ear. The high whistle woke her from her panicked flight, and she stopped abruptly. Where was she? Why? The trees around her were black and high, and the ground muddy.

She heard more shots, and shouting. With keen senses, she could identify her father's bass voice exploding within the ripping sound of gun shots. He was very close to her. Yellow lights filtered through the forest. She plunged forward.

A few meters ahead, the forest was cut sharply by a low fence. She climbed over it but slipped and fell flat to the frozen mud. She got up, kept on running. And then stopped.

*

Jerric squeezed off the last shots. Aiming carefully, squeezing, and aiming again. Two of his friends were lying on the ground, their dead eyes stunned. Jerric watched Erich out of the corner of his eye as he continued to fire aimless volleys from his light machine gun. He considered aiming at him, but he knew the real danger would come from another source. And Franz had pointed his gun at Jerric - and fired.

Jerric was surprised to see him miss at such close range. *Had he got so old too?* He was filled with light sorrow. But that did not stop him from aiming the gun again, to the center of Franz's chest, and squeezing the trigger. A red mushroom burst out of the chest of the best friend he had had in the last fifty years, and he fell back with a thud, shocked.

Only Erich was left.

Jerric turned to him - and felt his stomach tear.

151

After a long second, it also started to hurt. Jerric collapsed to the ground, dropped his gun, and a tall pile of mud stopped his landing.

Erich stopped shooting.

What was this madness? Erich did not understand. A moment ago he was on the winning side, a moment ago, he saw Jerric's gun aimed at the Jew's head - and then it was as if a demon had taken him over! It did not make any sense. It was not possible!

But it happened, and he responded, slowly but effectively.

And actually, he thought as he surveyed the crumbling Jerric, *he was not sorry*. He had dreamed of this moment for years. For years he had fantasized about the ways in which he would kill this cruel tyrant, who had humiliated him at every opportunity. For years he only dreamed of it - but now it had happened.

Jerric slowly writhed in pain. Erich smiled.

He turned his attention to the three men who were still standing near the graves.

Beautiful. Not one of the fools had thought of doing something to save themselves. They were shocked, all of them, and they would die the same way. But who first?

He pointed the rifle at Nicolas. Then at Isaiah. And then in slow motion at Jeremiah. *Yes. The Jew will die first.* He smiled again, and stroked the cold trigger with his finger.

A single shot pierced the night sky.

Requiem

"Give them according to their deeds, and according to the evil of their endeavors; give them after the work of their hands; render to them their desert." (Psalm 28:4)

For a moment the world went dark and silent.

Erich tried to see Jeremiah, but the place where the rabbi stood was only darkness now. He looked slightly to the right, and slightly to the left, and darkness still dominated his vision.

Then came the pain.

*

In front of Jeremiah's tortured eyes, Erich's body dropped to the ground, glimpsed only in fragmented movements. Slowly, in flash after flash of lightning, the old body fell down and folded onto the cemetery ground.

And behind him, in a perfect firing position, stood Eva.

Like an ancient goddess she stood there, lightning reflected off her cheeks. Rain dripped from her body, her long, straight hands, her locked elbows, her fingers gripping the rifle she had found near one of the bodies. She did not move. She did not tremble. She just stood there, knees slightly bent, her head erect, her eyes dark and with a sparkling Star of David around her neck.

She pulled the safety catch on and ran into the arms of her father.

Isaiah looked at them for a long time in happiness mixed with wonder. This girl could be his daughter, he knew, and he could almost feel her arms embracing him. There was something fascinating, mesmerizing, in Jeremiah and Eva, reunited again despite mountains of anger and resentment.

"This...is your daughter?" he asked finally

They broke apart, slowly. He looked at her. She was so familiar to him. So...familiar.

"You're... Isaiah." She looked at him somewhat dreamily.

The rain intensified around them, and a new burst of lightning spilled to the ground. Isaiah shook her wet hand, amazed.

"I feel like I know you. As if I've seen you somewhere..."

But when? And where? Both were from New York. Maybe they had met sometime. *Or was it just the family resemblance*, he thought. *And perhaps - but how did she get here?* A new answer, a stranger one at that, sprouted in his heart. But he brushed it aside. There must be a more rational explanation.

154

Behind them came a faint cough.

"Helena..."

Eva tensed, ready to react again, but she quickly relaxed when she saw Jerric flat on his back in the mud, his face white and frightened against the dark soil. He gasped, clutching his stomach.

Isaiah knelt beside him to better listen to the old wounded man.

"What did you say?

Jerric heavily lifted a shaking finger, pointing at Eva.

"Can't you see? That's...that's Helena... Helena Goldblum.

He tried to smile at her, a terrified distorted smile, but only coughed weakly again. For the first time in decades, Jerric was now afraid. His legs worked to distance himself from the vision, but only slipped in the mud. Jeremiah stepped towards him heavily, standing over him.

"This is my daughter, Eva Neumann."

What softness could not do, arrogance did. Jerric smiled, allowing blood to ooze from his mouth. He knew who he was seeing. And he knew why.

"No... Helena. Goldblum."

Nicolas touched Jeremiah's elbow. He knew who Helena Goldblum was.

"Helena," he whispered, "the one who put the letter in the box..."

Jerric coughed blood again, and nodded his head in wounded horror.

"Yes! Yes. Helena."

And again, a real, cold truth crawled in Isaiah's heart, this time to stay.

"Who are you? Who are you really?"

Jerric took a deep breath and looked at the mud.

*

This mud was only too familiar. So many years ago, in 1943 when the Russian front began to collapse, he began to suspect that the Third Reich would never rise. He detested the entire situation, and crossed the twenty meters that separated the commander's tent and the signaler's tent.

He did not even bother to return the salute of the soldier who greeted him at the door.

"Major Schroeder," said a young soldier who listened in on the radio, "they're coming!"

Yes, it was starting. He had known for several days that the Russians were on their way. Battered convoys retreating from the front left no room for doubt. The wave of the German invasion had stopped at Leningrad, and now they now retreated with great momentum to the borders of the old country, leaving a few puddles on the ground, leaving no way back.

His instructions were to hold the line, to fight to the last soldier, and to safeguard the withdrawal of other forces.

He and the nine men with him.

"They're coming!" screamed the young soldier, and the first whistle of a cannon shell interrupted his words, exploding near them. Mud and then more mud splattered everywhere.

Schroeder lifted the binoculars to his eyes. Something crawled over the hill on the eastern horizon: a Soviet tank. He counted one tank, two, three...

Another whistle and explosion came closer, hurling Schroeder to the mud. He cursed softly. They just were rabbits in a shooting range, that's what they were. Fight to the last soldier...what nonsense.

"Hans!" he shouted with a full throat. "Five minutes, no more! Take two jeeps, personal weapons only and battle rations! Nothing more! Head for the marshes! Move!"

*

When the Soviets got to the German position, they found fragments of brick and twisted metal. No bodies, however.

The German unit was already several kilometers from its former position, hidden by dense forest. He did not want to be caught by the Soviets - but even less did he want to come across 'friendly' German troops.

So he chose the more difficult route, paths that did not exist on the map, considered impassable, and to the best of his knowledge, not in the path of the Red Army's progress, nor the Nazis' retreat. He was an intelligence officer. He thought he knew this area very well.

After about an hour, he was lost.

Where he expected a high hill, there was a valley. Where there was supposed to be a river, he found extensive forest.

And where there was not supposed to be any settlement appeared ten stone cottages around three large trees.

Schroeder held the binoculars again. A young girl was hanging out laundry at one of the houses. Suddenly she raised her head and saw two jeeps on the ridge summit. She looked straight into the binoculars, then turned her head to one of the huts, and opened her mouth, apparently calling out.

After a few seconds, somebody came out of the cabin. Schroeder raised an eyebrow.

*

"We didn't think there were any more Jews left in Poland," Jerric grunted in pain, looking at Jeremiah's blank face. "But apparently those who lived so remote, so far away..."

His gazed moved to Eva.

"This was our opportunity to be saved."

*

When the jeep arrived at the village, most residents were already outside their huts. Most of them were old, some were wearing black clothes, typical black hats. The first of these, a short, relatively old man, stepped forward with a careful smile in his eyes.

Schroeder smiled back at him.

Then pulled the gun from his waistband, and shot him the head.

It was the signal for the soldiers behind him to fire a barrage. The startled crowd ahead was harvested almost without a reaction; most of the men were shot before they could turn and run.

"Only hit the men!" shouted Schroeder. "Do not touch women and children!"

It was over in less than a minute.

157

Two of the men had made it a few meters only to get shot in the back. Two children were also killed and injured. A child was shot in the head soon after. One woman was killed.

*

After a few hours, when the Soviets arrived, we were already prepared."

"What do you mean?"

Jerric sighed. He knew it would not be easy - but he did not know how hard it would be. He returned in his mind to that doomed day. He remembered every minute, every second. Recalled the tense minutes after the killings. Recalled how he put all the children in one room, one cottage, with Erich and a loaded gun. He recalled the screaming, the looks of hollow horror on the faces of the women, the panic that gripped their children, and the mothers desperately trying to calm them.

He recalled how he avoided killing other people, but did not refrain from pressing a threatening gun to the temple of one of the women. He recalled how he sent them to a place at the end of the village, the same place where he was dying now, to dig graves for their husbands.

He recalled how he sent the rest of his soldiers to destroy all Jewish tombstones and install makeshift wooden crosses above them. *Some of the old tombstones were still out there*, he thought suddenly, and admonished himself for being so careless. *How was it, during all these years, he hadn't made time to smash the whole place to smithereens?*

He recalled the first time he entered the cabin that served him for the next ten years. He recalled the awful simplicity - that sickened him initially - but taught him how to re-evaluate himself over the years. He recalled the rough wooden case in which he found his first clothes for his new life. *He was born twice*, that's how he always joked with himself. *The first time he came naked into the world. The second time he came dressed in a Jewish farmer's clothes.*

He recalled the moment at which the first Soviet tanks rose over the ridge.

*

158

The scream caught Schroeder trying on the Jew's clothes, the same one he killed a few hours ago. He threw aside his grey coat, hastily donning the torn clothes and (too small) shoes, and hobbled out.

The first Soviet tank began to move slowly down the hill, but close behind it appeared a faster jeep. Schroeder ran to the cabin which held all the women and children. He cocked his weapon and aimed it at the head of one of the children. One of the women shouted - but the rest just looked at him in horror. He handed his weapon to Franz, standing next to him and still wearing the Nazi uniform.

"*Rouse!*" he ordered the women. And they obeyed.

When the Soviet officer reached the village, he found all the women smiling and scattering flowers in the air. The men smiled, but remained in the background.

Then came that dreaded moment… with the little girl.

A little girl was sitting in the back of the jeep, and happily jumped out into the arms of one of the women there. With well-hidden horror he looked at the woman, who accepted the child at first, then turned away, almost pushing her back at the Soviet officer.

He saw the puzzled expression spreading over the face of the officer, and the bitter tears that suddenly seized the girl. He watched, in complete physical paralysis, how the officer tried to calm her, and how the woman was trying to maintain a distant facade.

He knew Franz was looking out the window, and was expecting gunfire at any moment. He tightened his grip on the service gun hidden in his pocket, knowing he could not win the war with it - but at least he could take a few Russians with him. He had already released the safety-

But then another woman walked forward, younger and more beautiful. She took the child in her hands, picked her up, hugged her and reassured her. The Soviet officer calmed down a little, but not completely.

"Kristzah," said the woman to the officer, smiling and nodding her head.

"Kristzah," he repeated, incredulously, and then repeated the name again, more convinced.

"It was Helena Goldblum." His breath was feeble now, and his voice weak.

Jerric's greying face contorted in pain more with each flash of lightning and a stream of black blood spewed out the corner of his mouth. He looked at Eva. She held the same gold pendant that had waited for her for fifty years.

"She was so beautiful. Exactly like you..."

"Murderer," hissed Jeremiah.

Jerric looked at him with dull, cold eyes.

"Those were different times, with different rules. We killed to live."

And he turned slowly to Isaiah. "You were right... it really is easier after you confess."

Isaiah did not respond. He was busy trying to understand what he was hearing, digesting what had happened here. Since meeting his twin brother, his view of the world had disintegrated slowly. The contact with the Poles, the search for old documents, the car... the attack on Jeremiah. All these things severely battered his delicate own world, which had been relatively protected until the last few weeks.

And now... this.

The shots still rang in his ears, and his body was very tired. The long minutes since he had stopped digging cooled his body, and the freezing rain coming down made him tremble. Confession? It was the most inappropriate time to confess. Still, a man lay before him, in his last moments on earth, and confessed the cardinal sins known to man. *Could he refuse him?* He decided not to.

"And what else?" he asked in a tired and distant voice.

"More? There is much to tell. As you may have noticed, this village is so remote, that no one was interested in it until long after the war was over. We had time to learn Polish, to learn to milk cows, to plow the land... we became Poles. When the Soviets came to this village it was all ready with a new story, with new residents."

"And the women? The children?"

"Dead. They are all dead."

Jerric did not add anything, and no one dared to ask for more. The old man's breathing continued to be tortuous, his eyes fixed on Eva,

160

and blood oozed from his mouth. Finally it was Jeremiah who broke the silence.

"And what about us?"

Jerric was silent. He sighed slightly and lowered his eyes to the floor. And remained silent.

"What about the twins?" Jeremiah asked again, annoyed. "You didn't mention us. Why?"

"You were not yet born, then."

"Who was our mother?"

Jerric was able to smile crookedly. He looked at Eva.

"Your mother was the most beautiful woman in the village. A lot like your daughter, very similar. She was also a very smart woman."

"What was her name?"

Jerric was trying to get his fingers into his coat pocket, but the hand was too weak, and would not move the whole way. Jerric groaned in pain.

"Pocket..." he gestured.

Isaiah bent over, reaching out – in some disgust – into the inner pocket of Jerric's coat, and pulled out the metal box, that till not long ago, had been buried in the ground. He opened it.

A strange, magnetic pull lit up in Eva's eyes. Almost instinctively she put out her hand, and grabbed the golden locket. She looked at it as if spellbound, stroking it with her hand. Three intense lighting forks, one by one, lit the sky up behind her with a white light. She lifted the locket to her mouth, tasted it with her tongue and put it close to her heart.

Her fingers embraced it.

Her fingers, with blind skill, found the hidden mechanism.

After fifty years of darkness, the pendant opened to the night's light.

It was a photo. A very old one, black and white, printed on thick paper with jagged edges. A simple photo of a young couple. A Jewish couple. The husband was a young man, with a hooked nose and a beard. And the woman - Helena. Helena Goldblum.

Eva's black pupils widened to full size. They were like two peas in a pod, from the curve of their smiles and eyebrows to their hairstyle. Weakness took over her entire body, but in a complete contrast, she was filled with a powerful and strange vitality. A sense of completion. For one full moment, fire burned in Eva's body, and she felt fulfilled... even joyful.

For one full moment she felt a bright aura surrounding her, radiating a soothing heat... a weird touch, a relaxing caress. For a moment, Eva felt how her grandmother's eyes watched her sons, and a maternal love, waiting for a generation, sparked at full capacity - and then dissipated slowly.

Eva looked at the picture of Helena and stared back at her, smiling across generations. After a few seconds, she handed the locket to her father and uncle. For the first time in fifty years, they looked at their mother.

"You killed her husband when you came here," said Isaiah.

"Yes."

"I mean, she... was she pregnant?"

Jerric shook his head.

Something broke in Isaiah's heart. Different parts of the puzzle began to fit in suddenly, and the image it made was worse than hell. He did not want to be there. He did not want to know. He did not want to. Just did not.

"Who was our father?" he asked in a trembling voice.

Jerric did not answer.

"Who is - was - our father?"

"He was not the Holy Spirit, I can assure you, *father*."

"Who was he?"

The scream became a cry, a bitter one. But Jerric saw and heard nothing. Everything was black in his eyes, pulsating black as the blood drained from his body. He had no more than ten minutes to live, he knew. Would he pass them in silence? Part of him longed for it. To s*leep... to die... perhaps to dream?*

No, he did not want to dream.

He was afraid to dream, even. So he opened his eyes, breathed again, spat out the blood that had accumulated in his mouth, and began to croak his last words.

"She was the most beautiful girl in the village. And I am... I was the commander."

162

His voice trailed off again, full of regrets. Eva closed the locket and slipped it in her pocket. Jeremiah, who had remained silent for several minutes, brought himself to speak again.

"And you killed her."

Jerric looked at him.

"A year after we had the twins, it was time to start eliminating the women and children. The war was about to end, and there was no more reason to keep them alive." He breathed raggedly and continued.

"Helena...she knew what was coming. She was a wise woman. She begged me to let the babies live...she begged me. The morning of the assassination, I deliberately left the door unlocked..."

*

The small hut was dimly lit by the rays of the spring sun which made their way through the dirty square window. They landed partly on a rough wooden table, partly on the armless chair.

On the side wall was a wooden double bed, a little more polished than the table and chairs. Next to it stood a small closet and on it was a large wicker basket. And in the basket: twins, babies, less than a year old.

Helena Goldblum made her bed without a smile. She had not smiled a lot in the past year, and her natural beauty had become Venusian, almost poetic. Her black hair, worn loose until the last year was now permanently tied, bound with a linen string and laid on the back of her neck. From the corner of her eye she looked at her two children, the only two reasons that had prevented her from committing suicide so far.

She smiled at them, seeing their little eyes following her. She simply adored them. She lived for them. Was this the reason Schroeder let this pregnancy go on? She did not know, but suspected so. The last year had been an ongoing nightmare. She still remembered the last moments of her life with her husband... until Schroeder shot him.

She knew the war was over. She knew that the Germans had lost. A government official came to the village a few weeks ago and recorded the number of people in Bielisk... In Nabradosky, that is. She had to say Nabradosky. She so wanted to do something, say something - but was afraid. Schroeder (now known as Jerric) told her exactly what he would do to his own children to silence her.

And she hated being in the only place in the world still occupied by the Nazis, hated to be occupied herself - desecrated and unclean. If not for the children she would have run away a long time ago... if not for the children.

She looked at them again, dipping into their large, innocence eyes.

Then, from outside the cabin, she heard curses in German and a high scream (she recognized the voice. It was Sarah Feldman, Leah's mother... poor little Kristzah) and a shot.

Sarah's voice was cut off.

More shots, then commotion and commands.

Helena ran to the window, scared. *Had it started?*

Erich crossed the clearing in front of her to the cabin that he made his own quarters (with Rachel, whom he raped regularly), a sub-machine gun in his hand. He opened the door and just started shooting inside. She saw how he laughed. A few shouts were audible from inside, some were of children. After a few seconds they died down.

Erich turned and Helena moved away from the window, panicked.

Her heart was beating fast. It had started. For one reason or another, Schroeder had decided that today he would complete the work of the cleansing the Jews, killing anyone in the village. She looked desperately at the twins. Was this what she had suffered so much for? Is it why she had buried the incriminating documents which she had stolen from his drawer at the beginning of the winter?

Why now? She knew that new Polish officials would visit the village soon. Just a few more weeks before she could tell the whole truth - and get out of this hell. Just a few weeks to go - *but Schroeder, of course, knew that as well as she did.* And therefore he would not give her those weeks. She was about to die. And the twins with her.

Really?

Without much hope, she went to the door and tried the knob. A surprise: the door opened! Strange. *It was not typical of Schroeder.* She left it open just a slit, grabbed a thick woolen blanket, covered the twins with it, took the big basket, and began to make her way out.

At the door she paused again and took a deep breath.

She put the basket on the floor, and approached the bed itself. With great effort she moved it, knelt behind it and began to feel the rough bricks that made up the wall. After a few seconds one of them came free and fell to the floor, leaving behind a dark hole in the wall.

Helena reached into the niche and pulled out a delicate gold chain, her tiny pendant in the form of a golden star. She looked at it for a second, then quickly put it round her neck and charged out, the twins' basket in her hands.

*

"I couldn't shoot her. I don't know why," lied Schroeder as he looked into Eva's eyes.

She was so much like her, he thought. But another look into the dark embers that shone in Eva's face told him that at least at this moment, she was not just *like* her. She just... *was* her. She had come to haunt him, to watch as he died, as he had watched her die.

Suddenly, he was afraid.

He looked at Isaiah and was afraid. His death was near, and the scent of his own blood burned in his nostrils. Soon the wolves would come, he knew, and take him away down under. Helena continued to look at him from the eyes of her granddaughter.

*

Just as she had looked, at that moment when she had burst out of the cabin, her eyes blinking in the strong light.

Schroeder looked at her through the crosshair of the gun, as he half-hid behind a tree. Except for the rifle it was impossible to distinguish him from all the other Polish peasants, from the shabby shoes to a new belly that he had grown, and the unshaven beard.

The gun was cocked. Helena was at the center of his crosshairs, but the gun muzzle remained quiet.

He looked at her, as her legs struck out, taking her in the opposite direction. First right, then left, directly at him, and then, with much thought, far away, into the forest.

165

He followed her with his gun, his finger stroking the trigger.

Then another woman entered his field of vision, running in the same direction. The gun thundered, and the woman fell, splashing red from her shoulder.

Helena screamed and broke into a gallop.

Death began to run after her.

*

"She knew I was behind her. She came to me and stood before me. She kept looking me in the eyes till the end."

Schroeder tried to say something more, but was stopped by a wet, bloody cough.

Jeremiah grabbed his brother's arm gently, pressing it lightly. Isaiah was the weaker of the two of them, he knew now. And himself? Something in Judaism had prepared him for this. Somewhere, he innately understood that this story had lived within him all his life.

"It was her grave that we saw. Correct?"

The rain continued to wash the cold ground, but the lightning at last moved away and disappeared and with it went the thunder, and Jerric's voice.

Jeremiah asked again, "When we saw you at the stones – was it her grave?"

But Jerric still did not answer.

Nor breathed.

*

Under the persistent cloud of rain they buried the bodies in the open graves, maintaining absolute silence. Nicolas and Eva did most of the work, while Jeremiah tried to rest in the vehicle and Isaiah did his best to keep him warm.

When the work ended and they went back to Nabradosky the horizon was already starting to brighten. A new day, somewhat darker, was born. None of them smiled.

After four hot showers and a short breakfast, they were ready to leave this death town for good. While the others were packing, Isaiah went out to return the boxes of documents to the town hall, which would open in half an hour.

Maybe it was fatigue. Maybe he just did not notice.

But as Isaiah finished unloading the fourth box, something blunt struck his temple and he fell to the ground. For a moment he thought it was a car door carelessly opened, but the second blow made him realize something else was going on.

The kick that smashed into his mouth finally convinced him. He felt broken teeth with his tongue.

Stood over him, a little frightened but determined, stood three shaven-headed teenagers, red-eyed from a night fueled by alcohol. Pavel's hand held his iron rod.

"Maybe we should burn him, he's not dead!"

Pavel continued to kick Isaiah, out of fear more than any other reason. He could not believe his eyes. *It was the same Jew that he'd killed a couple of days ago - but unscathed, without even a scratch! And dressed...*

"It can't be him," said one of the boys behind him. "He had a beard."

"And he's dressed like a priest," added another.

"Look!" Pavel shouted hysterically. "It is, I tell you! He shaved his beard off and disguised himself as a priest! Jew Devil!"

Pavel stopped kicking and looked closely at the bleeding Isaiah. He tried to remember the face of the bearded Jew that he was sure he had killed a few (few?) days ago. *Same nose... same eyes, the same features. There was no doubt – it was the same person. The same devil.*

Isaiah tried to get up, and Pavel jumped back in fear.

"Look - he recognizes me!" Pavel was on the verge of hysteria.

"Where the signs of the beating?" the idiots behind him continued to ask him.

"I don't know! Jewish... wizard! Maybe he drank blood. I don't know!"

Somehow, Isaiah pulled himself up on his hands and rose up. He looked at them with dazed eyes. He was in pain, but he was still conscious and still not broken.

"Who... who are you...?"

Pavel shivered and crossed himself. His grandfather told him about this... blood-drinking Jews that change shape and can catch you while

167

you sleep. He had not believed these stories... but maybe he was wrong?

"You see? Same voice. Same face… and now he's disguised himself as a priest!"

In a rush of courage, he tore Isaiah's clerical collar from his neck and threw it on the ground, stamping and spitting on it.

"*Zyd*!" he screamed, and launched a harsh kick to his face.

Something in his madness managed to infect the others, not because they thought he was serious, not because they believed in what he believed. It was just simple and easy. They were tired, but not too tired. And drunk, far too drunk.

So they closed in on Isaiah, a ring of darkness around the *Zyd* priest. And broke the fuse of his life with fierce blows.

*

The Jewish cemetery in Brooklyn had never opened its doors to such a large number of officials of the Catholic Church. They walked in silence, red and white caps on their heads, some in robes, some in standard attire.

They moved silently in front of the open casket, honoring their fallen fellow.

Jeremiah did not pass in front of the coffin.

Instead, he kept to himself, alone in the purity room, repeating his words, repeating his words over and over again.

Finally, there was a knock on the door and he came out.

Eva met him outside the building, the golden locket visible around her neck. She took his hand and supported him along the long path that led to the grave. He had been that way hundreds of times. It had never been longer nor harder.

The little whispers surrounding Isaiah's body faded when Jeremiah crossed through the sea of people. They parted before him, some to the right and some to the left, looking fearfully over the signs of bruises evident on his face. His right hand dangled in a sling, and his left foot was clad in a cast. And yet he went forward, stable, but heavily.

Hundreds of people watched him.

168

And he began to cry out softly.

"My brother, Isaiah. You are no longer with me. You were not with me for fifty-two years, but the short time we were together - it was like eons.

"My brother Isaiah. I never knew you as other people here did. I did not have a chance. But, nevertheless, I knew you better than anyone else. Because you were my twin brother. My only brother, as I was your only brother.

"My brother Isaiah, the earth trembles beneath me. I wanted to be with you longer. Love you more. I bring you today to a grave, and a part of me dies with you today.

"My brother Isaiah! You lived your life as a Christian. Grew up as a Christian. Studied as a Christian. Lived as a Christian. But were murdered - as a Jew."

A long silence hovered the cemetery, controlling the sounds of the wind, even the cooing pigeons. And out of the silence came words which grew rapidly and tore the skyline.

"El malei rachamim..."

*

Hours later his red eyes stared at him from the mirror in his bathroom.

It had been a long day and now it was over.

Jeremiah opened the hot water tap and let it flow freely. He put his good hand under the stream, feeling how his fingers heated up to the point of discomfort, and balanced them out with a little cold water.

He gasped slightly, took off his yarmulke, and laid it gently beside him. From the bottom drawer he slowly drew a pair of sharp scissors, usually used by the girls.

He held the scissors to his throat.

And started cutting off his beard.

<u>Epilogue</u>

First, I would like to apologize.

Sad stories are not my favorite. I prefer bright storylines, Hollywood plots, with a happy ending and facile catharsis. Yet, this book was stronger than me. Despite my ambitions, I could not write it any other way, full of humor and self-awareness. We'll see, maybe in the next book.

So I apologize if I made you think, cry, angry. I did not mean to, really. This book wrote itself, from a certain point. It took on a life of its own, and went in directions that surprised me too.

There is much to say about this book, actually.

So here is this invitation - a personal invitation to comment, speak, and talk to me. You did me the honor of reading the book, and I appreciate that more than you can imagine.

I'd love to hear from you. Please leave me a review on my Amazon page.

Regards,
L. L. Fine

ABOUT THE AUTHOR

L. L. Fine lives in a small town in Israel, and is taught humility and manners by his three charming children, loving wife, demanding cats, noisy neighbors and unsatisfied readers.

For more information, and books, go to www.LLFine.com

CPSIA information can be obtained
at www.ICGtesting.com
Printed in the USA
LVHW010323070720
659945LV00017B/1264

9 781493 710362